Three Trips

to

Hell

John Kildea

HERITAGE BOOKS
2019

HERITAGE BOOKS

AN IMPRINT OF HERITAGE BOOKS, INC.

Books, CDs, and more—Worldwide

For our listing of thousands of titles see our website
at
www.HeritageBooks.com

Published 2019 by
HERITAGE BOOKS, INC.
Publishing Division
5810 Ruatan Street
Berwyn Heights, Md. 20740

Copyright © 2019 John Kildea

Heritage Books by the author:
No Names, No Faces, No Pain: A Voice from Vietnam
Three Trips to Hell
Three Under A Tree

International Standard Book Number
Paperbound: 978-0-7884-5810-1

PART ONE

INTRODUCTIONS, PLEASE

Chapter One

The Reunion

Imagine, if you would, just for a moment, please, four old guys sitting in a bar. It's an older neighborhood place with a flickering neon beer sign in its tiny front window. In addition, there's that miserable brown paint you see everywhere you look peeling literally from every square foot of the outside woodwork. The front screen door is tattered and torn in numerous places, and though the hinges appear to be lacking a few screws, overall, it's miraculously functional.

Inside, perched high on their stools, the images of the old timers reflect perfectly from the typical taproom mirror, covering one wall from the top of the bar to the ceiling, and from one end of the bar to the other. As you would suspect, filling three or four shelves of varying heights in front of the mirror, a hundred or so bottles of liquor of various colors, shapes and sizes.

A full day's growth of beard on each man speaks perhaps to the time of day; the slouch in their shoulders, probably the same. Empty whiskey glasses, half full beer mugs, dollar bills and a variety of change scattered about the bar indicates these men have been here for a while, obviously with no intention of leaving anytime soon.

Like most men their age, conversations revolve around their health, doctor's visits, grandchildren and an occasional movie seen with the wife. Though a jukebox playing in the background makes it necessary for them to sometimes repeat themselves, each, for the most part, speaks softly and slowly, clearly and calmly.

When you really begin to listen to these guys you quickly realize they've gathered here, not simply to catch up on the latest gossip and to renew old friendships, but rather to share, perhaps for the last time, utterly unimaginable moments of pain from each of their lives.

You get the feeling they're speaking of war, and because of their ages, assume it to be World War ll. When you overhear words such as beriberi, bayoneting, decapitation, and dysentery, you become downright certain that's the case.

Each man has his own story, yet all are strikingly similar. Each begins several hours after the bombing of Pearl Harbor on December 7th in 1941 when the Japanese suddenly turned their wrath toward Luzon and Corregidor in the Philippine Islands. What was once a paradise military assignment for all four instantly became enshrouded in the fog of war with strafing, bombings, and eventually an invasion by tens of thousands.

As an innocent bystander, it now becomes nearly impossible to relive with these fellows the horrors of their capture; making the Bataan Death March, their treatment at the hands of such a murderous foe in filthy and infested prisoner of war camps, and enduring the final insult of being crammed aboard the so-called Japanese "Hell Ships".

If you're not a history buff or at least seventy-five to eighty years of age, you probably know little of this whole affair. For the sake of accuracy, therefore, we'll let these guys themselves give you the facts. Share with us, if you would, their horrendous "Three Trips to Hell".

Chapter Two

1ST. Lieutenant Jack Kaster

That afternoon we did in fact spend a fair amount of time discussing how fast my prostate was growing and the state of the economy, but most of the conversation that day was a rehash of the days we spent as prisoners of the Japanese during World War ll. Again, if you're younger than seventy-five or eighty years of age, you might have some knowledge of the World War II, know even less of the Bataan Death March, and have never even heard of "Hell Ships". Well, the four of us will try to shed a bit of light on all three subjects, and how we just happened to be involved in all of them.

Before I go any further I suppose something about myself and my background might be useful. Then a bit about what led up to the four of us being placed in a line with seventy-five-thousand Filipino and American prisoners, stretching some sixty-five miles on the Bataan Death March might also be helpful.

Me? I was born in 1913, if you can believe that's possible, in El Paso, Texas. My name is John Lafferty Kaster but my friends call me Jack. Along with my brother James, I spent my early years living with our folks above a funeral parlor from which they owned and operated a casket manufacturing company. Of course, with its prime customers just downstairs, I'm told the company did very well. During those years, though I remember little, I was getting into all sorts of trouble with friends and earning what could only be called piss poor grades.

That behavior and those grades resulted in my beginning high school at a boarding school known as the New Mexico Military Institute just outside Roswell, New Mexico. Military to the core, the day began standing at attention with the raising of the flag and ended with its being lowered at sunset. In between there were many classes broken up by a multitude of boring and very tiring marching drills. As you might suspect, I did carry a bit of resentment for being sent hundreds of miles from home for what I considered a minor problem with my attitude.

Regardless, whether it was the military regime, or because of being separated from my so-called friends, my grades over time slowly crept up to a bit above average. My frame of mind also changed considerably. With these improvements, it came as no surprise when my folks signed me up to attend junior college at the Institute. I had little means to resist.

Those two years went by quickly. In 1932 I graduated, not only with my associate's degree, but with a commission as a 2nd. Lieutenant in the Army Officer Reserve Corps. Times, they were a changing!

The Institute, as its name implies, served as a prep school for those interested in moving on into any of the military academies. Though my grades had moved upward I was by no means interested in doing so. My academic achievements did, however, allow me to transfer to the University of Arizona in Tucson where I graduated in 1934. With a BA and BS in Business Administration I gladly accepted a position to manage a portion of the business at home.

In 1935 the business merged with a fellow named Earl Maxon and a full complement of embalmers. A second funeral parlor opened and both became Kaster and Maxon Funeral Homes. Mr. Maxon served as president of the company, my mother as VP.

Dad became the president of the casket company, and brother James, the secretary-treasurer. By 1938 I had married Susan, a beautiful girl from Massachusetts. Almost immediately she became treasurer of the casket company while I served as VP. Life was really getting good!

♣♣♣♣♣♣

Despite the activity in our lives, unbelievably I decided to remain in the reserves. That decision bit me in the butt. Not that I wouldn't have been drafted anyway, but in June of 1941 my outfit, the 7th Materials Squadron, was called to active duty.

After a very long, hot summer as basic trainees at Fort Bliss, Texas, we were taken to San Francisco, and placed on barges that carried us to Angeles, a small island just off the coast. Here we spent a week processing, getting shots, preparing wills, drawing weapons and all that stuff to get us ready to go overseas.

When all our ducks were in a row, we were placed on a rusty old steamer and told we were heading for the Philippines. Specifically, we were heading for Fort Stoltenberg, adjacent to Clark Field, about fifty miles north of Manila. I was now a 1st Lieutenant, a company commander, and a supply officer who would provide support for some of the tens of thousands of Army, Air Force, Marines and Navy personnel on the islands.

Seemed to us that Uncle Sam was placing thousands of troops in offensive positions that might be needed in case the Japanese decided to attack the Philippines. Suddenly the future appeared a tad bit shaky.

Chapter Three

Major Wendall Swanson, M.D.

My life and trip to the Philippines was like that of Jack's in many ways, but very different in many others – our fondness of academics being one.

Brought into this world in April of 1904, I was born in Georgia but reared in Tennessee with my two brothers and two sisters. I was the third born of five and my name is Wendall Fleet Swanson. The Wendall came about because for some reason our folks gave each of us kids a first name that began with the letter "W". The Fleet, my mother's maiden name, was given as my middle name; apparently a common practice at the time.

My Dad was a supply clerk for a copper mine most of his life; my Mom a grammar school teacher. Because of her watchful eye, my grades in both grade school and high school were excellent. That continued as I attended Maryville College in eastern Tennessee in the mid-1920s. Eventually I transferred to the University of Tennessee in Memphis where, while working as a clerk in a drug store, I attained both my bachelors and my medical degrees.

During this time, I began dating a young lady from Arkansas who was living with her sister and working as an operator for

AT&T in Memphis. Her name was Maude Prentice, and in November of 1930, with me still a student, we married.

Upon graduating, I enlisted in the Army with a promise of an internship, followed by a surgical residency with an emphasis on trauma. We didn't know it at the time, but Uncle Sam was truly planning!

Maude and I enjoyed five wonderful years at Fitzsimmons General Hospital in Denver Colorado. In 1940, upon completing my residency, I was proudly promoted to the rank of Major.

When I received orders to report to Fort Mills Hospital on Corregidor in the Philippine Islands, however, we felt it best for Maude to return home with her parents. Corregidor is the largest of four smaller islands lying just south of Luzon, the main island three miles from the strategically important Manila Bay.

In addition to the hospital, Corregidor held fifty-six pieces of coastal artillery. The remaining three islands maintained fewer guns. It was obvious that the purpose of all four islands combined was to protect the entrance to the bay and its access to Manila.

In December of 1941 the Japanese let loose with their attack on Pearl Harbor, decimating the Pacific Fleet. Ten hours later they turned their attention towards Clark Air Field on Luzon. Initial bombardments focused on medium and heavy bombers brought to the Philippines in anticipation of just such attacks by the enemy. Now, neatly lined up on runways and unattended while their aircrews ate lunch, thirty-six were destroyed.

From patients we treated we learned that simultaneous attacks on other fields by Japanese Zeros destroyed all but four P-40 escort fighters on the ground, taxing for takeoff, or in combat. At one other field, every single P-35 fighter was burned to the ground. Indeed, World War II had officially begun!

On the first day of the bombardment of Clark Air Field the incessant aerial attacks rendered most runways useless due to the numerous bomb craters created. By December 11th the mere seventeen surviving B-17s and twenty P-40s and P-35s abandoned Clark Field and escaped to Australia in their attempt to fight yet another day. Likewise, submarines, the only naval vessels still at the Cavite Naval Facility, also made their break for safety.

While attacks continued on Luzon over the weeks that followed, it wasn't until December 29th that Corregidor was finally bombed. Over the course of the first two hours the Japanese destroyed several barracks, the Officers Club, the Naval fueling station and the hospital. After that, until the end of January, raids became infrequent and damage minimal.

During the lull in the action, all of us moved quickly to improve our situation. The Navy placed all their resources on rebuilding the fueling station. Homeless service members were assigned to bunk with others. With the hospital destroyed, although ours was a unique problem, it was easily resolved.

The Malinta Complex was a huge tunnel bored deep into the rock of Corregidor. Built by the Army Corps of Engineers using obsolete equipment rented from local gold miners, utilizing some one thousand convicts from Bilibid prison in Manila for labor, it ran eight-hundred and thirty feet deep, twenty-four feet wide, and eighteen feet high. Branching off from the main shaft, thirteen on one side and eleven on the other, were additional one-hundred and sixty-foot-long lateral tunnels.

Used originally as a bomb proof shelter for personnel and storage of supplies and equipment, it also provided space for the offices of General Douglas MacArthur and other high-ranking officers, such as Lt. General Jonathan Wainwright, their staffs and families.

Chosen quickly for its ideal protection of patients, salvageable beds, medicine cabinets, x-ray machines and all other medical nursing equipment were gathered from the bombed-out Fort Mills Hospital and moved into the tunnels. Needed supplies and equipment were procured from Sternberg Hospital in Manila or bought from local suppliers.

The laterals were converted to hospital wards, labs, space for the well-equipped operating rooms, a laundry and all other departments necessary to run the hospital. Finally, staff were assigned living quarters in the remaining lateral tunnels. Needless to say, the mental anxiety concerning our physical welfare was greatly relieved.

While Corregidor had been spared from constant enemy attacks during December of 1941 and January of 1942, the men on Luzon were taking quite a beating. On December 23rd and 24th, some forty-three-thousands of Japan's finest troops landed, supported by tanks and artillery to the north of Manila. At the same time, another seven thousand troops from the same division with the same support were landing at the southern end of the island.

MacArthur had planned on placing some one hundred thousand reserve troops in the Philippines. He achieved less than half of that goal. He had requested newer M1 Garrard rifles to replace the aging World War 1 Enfield's equipping his forces. Congress refused his request. His divisions had only 20% of their artillery requirements. It would be kind to say the general was ill prepared for the war. With these critical shortfalls in men, rifles, and artillery, the Japanese easily sliced through our front lines, at the same time gobbling up supplies previously intended to be used by troops during the defense of the islands.

Such supplies consisted of ammunition, medicines, blankets, sun helmets and most importantly, rations and water. Because of the losses, men on both Luzon and Corregidor were immediately placed on half rations, then quarter rations, and reduced rations once again. Soon, men working in the tunnels were reduced to skin and bones, malnourished and dehydrated. Men in the field were half-starved, now easy targets for jungle diseases such as beriberi and malaria.
With more and more American and Filipino soldiers ill and finding it difficult to fight, troops on Luzon began retreating toward the Bataan Peninsula, the only ground thus far not occupied by the Japanese.

In a frantic move to survive, the retreating soldiers salvaged what supplies they could, food and water atop their list. Day and night goods meant to sustain forty-five thousand troops for six months were sent by barge onto the peninsula. Suddenly, eighty thousand troops and twenty-six thousand civilians flooded the jungle retreat as the Japanese were sealing off the flow of refugees.

On Corregidor, bombing resumed once again, and Japanese soldiers invaded the island. The defenders, mostly Marines and sailors, held their own, however, and inflicted heavy casualties. With the remaining heavy guns, they succeeded in knocking many Japanese planes from the sky.

Interestingly, by March of 1942 the Japanese had figured out that if they placed oxygen in their bombers they could fly just a little higher than the range of the anti-aircraft batteries on Corregidor. Immediately, heavier bombardment began. Simultaneously, foot soldiers established beachheads and reinforced them with the customary tanks and artillery.

More and more guns were put out of commission by the bombers and Japanese forces soon began to push defenders back toward the Malinta tunnel. U.S. submarines arrived under cover of darkness to bring in mail and more weapons. Most importantly, they removed gold and silver, top secret documents, and high-ranking officials and their families, including General MacArthur.

"Dugout" Doug, as he would soon come to be known, promised remaining forces, "Help is on the way from the United States. Thousands of troops and hundreds of planes are being dispatched". He told us supplies would serve us until we were relieved, but he gave no timetable. Most men believed him. Many, however, thought otherwise.

Chapter Four

1st. Lieutenant Bill Bianchi

Hi! I'm Bill Bianchi, and I'm the third of the pub dwellers. My first name is really Willibald, so you can understand why I go by Will or Bill. Anyway, I'd like to take this opportunity to do as Jack and Doctor Swanson have done, and tell you a little about myself, my family and how we guys all came to cross paths.

New Ulm, a small town in south central Minnesota, was the place of my birth in early 1915. With a population of about six thousand it was known statewide for its many well-run poultry farms and locally for its true sense of community. When they talk about towns where everybody knows everyone else, this is one of them.

♣♣♣♣♣♣

I was the second of five born to my parents. My father used to say he and I were badly outnumbered by my mother and four sisters. I tended to agree.

We were a very strict Catholic family in the early years of our upbringing. Dad was an active member of the Knights of Columbus and the Saint Anthony's Society. Mom was a volunteer at the rectory. As kids, we attended Saint Anthony elementary and Cathedral high school. Having kids from a good Catholic family going to a public school would not have been kosher.

Mom worked making pastry in a bakery in town for as many years as I can remember. Dad worked as a shipping clerk at a local mill for over thirty years. Bored with the daily grind, he and a friend finally quit and opened a grocery store. With the Great Depression looming around the corner it all came crashing down around their ears.

Dad came bouncing back, mortgaged everything we had, and bought a dairy farm with forty cows and a chicken hatchery. He named it Bianchi Holstein and Leghorn Farm. He was in heaven!

One Saturday morning in early April of 1932, dad drove Mom to town to shop and visit with the ladies. About noon she called to check on the progress of the girls who were preparing lunch, and to talk with Dad about a pick-up time.

About an hour earlier Magdalene told my father she had spotted a dog running loose near the brooder houses. With several chicks having recently been killed, he was certain he had the guilty culprit cornered. He grabbed several shells and his shotgun, loading it as he went out the door.

With Mom now on the phone, I volunteered to run and fetch Dad. When I reached the fence line at the hatcheries, Dad was lying on his back on the other side of the wire. He had an obvious gunshot wound to his right upper chest. I knew he was dead.

The coroner determined Dad's pant leg had gotten caught on a broken wire as he climbed over the fence. He apparently dropped his shotgun, butt first onto the ground. With the gun facing upward and his chest pressing on the muzzle, the gun misfired from the force of it hitting the ground. Dad's death was ruled simply a tragic accident.

Life became very difficult without my father. I had friends, certainly, but you talk to your Dad about things that help you grow up. The guys talked about things that tended to slow that process.

Now being the only man in the house, I felt obligated to help with the farm. A few months later, at the end of my high school sophomore year, I dropped out of school. I did continue to attend classes at night and on weekends all year round and was finally awarded my high school diploma three years later.

During this time, I joined the Junior ROTC. Upon graduation, I was awarded a full academic scholarship to South Dakota State University. It would pay books and tuition for all four years. In exchange, I agreed to serve eight years as an officer with the U.S. Army – four years on active duty, four years in the reserves.

In 1935, with me going to college and Josephine, my sister, engaged to be married, Mom realized that she could not run the farm with three teenage girls. She frequently spoke of the "empty nest" and the need for her to move on with her life without my father. Encouraged by all of us by the end of spring she put the Bianchi farm on the selling block.

Within months the "Holstein" side of the business was sold. A few months later, with the help of God, the hatcheries, the house and the land was snatched up "lock, stock, and barrel".

With a nifty little profit, Mom and the girls moved into a beautiful, though in need of minor repairs, large Victorian style house on the edge of town. Mary Louise and Germain, nineteen and nine, respectfully, were still in school. Josephine had fallen in love, gotten married, fallen out of love, gotten divorced, and moved back home. She had started to attend Saint Theresa College in Winona, Minnesota with hopes of becoming a teacher. Magdalene was now happily married to a farmer living not far from Mom.

Upon graduation in 1939, I, too, returned home to await my commission and orders for my initial assignment. To earn my keep, during the warmer months I painted the outside of the house. During the colder months, I painted the inside.

Finally, in January of 1940 I received my commission as a 2nd. Lieutenant. My family and I were proud as punch! At the same time, I received orders to report to basic training. Having a gut feeling that war was eminent, I volunteered for foreign duty so that I might be nearer the action if my intuition was correct.

Following basic training my first assignment was as the Commander of D Company of the Philippine Scouts, 45th Infantry, in Bagac on the Bataan Peninsula in the Philippine Islands. Here, following extensive training in weapons and munitions, battlefield tactics, leadership and much more, I would be expected to be able not only to teach new recruits, but also to lead them into battle. I could not have been more pleased with my assignment.

The next year and a half was not only interesting but unbelievably educational. For a kid from the Midwest to travel halfway around the world proved overwhelming. To learn the customs of another people in a new land, likewise, most challenging. Practicing fighting was downright eerie.

During this time, I received my "on- the-job" training from three top notch NCOs passing on their knowledge and expertise to me and hundreds of others destined to become scouts. My leadership skills had been tested to the point that we were certain I could lead these men into battle. All who had been trained thus far were scattered about Luzon ready to defend their homeland.

By now we all knew that the Japanese had wreaked havoc on most of the Pacific Fleet at Pearl Harbor on December 7th of 1941. Now, they could no longer be of assistance to other American forces elsewhere in the world. The only saving grace at Pearl Harbor that day was that the aircraft carriers with their priceless cargo of planes were out at sea on maneuvers at the time of the attack.

Within hours of Pearl Harbor, the Japanese carried their assault to the Commonwealth of the Philippines, a protectorate of the U.S. Here they bombed airfields including Clark Field, the Naval station, barracks, the hospital and anything else American they could line up in their bombsites.

So, why all the death and destruction on the part of the Japanese? Perhaps it was just a deadly game of "King of the Hill". There were more practical reasons.

Because Japan had no natural resources of her own on any of its islands, she had been obligated to buy them on the world market. Now because of bad economic times she found that more difficult. She decided to invade other countries such as China or Manchuria, and simply steal them.

Eventually, because of such actions, the United States, Great Britain, and the Netherlands decided to initiate a total embargo of the oil Japan usually purchased from them. Without oil, Japan could never survive.

So, with the Pacific Fleet crippled, along with eliminating further interference from the United States and by having captured the Philippines, Japan looked a bit to the south for their next move. Overtaking a few of the islands in the Dutch Indies would easily provide Japan with enough oil for the homeland and the war effort for many years to come.

Doctor Swanson spoke earlier of the first month or two of the Japanese occupation of Luzon and Corregidor. Mention was made that the Americans had gathered food, water, ammunition, and other supplies and placed them in thousands of crates and hidden them on the periphery of the islands. Here, if the war began and supply lines were cut off, they were intended to sustain approximately eighty thousand American and Filipino troops for at least six months.

Unfortunately, when the enemy invaded they located practically every crate that had been squirreled away in caves, churches, schools, and even on the beaches. The ammunition was antiquated and unusable. They cared little for American style food, and did not want to burden themselves with the extra weight. Every single crate found its way to the bottom of the ocean!

Aware of the "gold mine" they had discovered, the Japanese became very patient. American and Filipino troops, weakened by disease and malnutrition, were no longer a match for the enemy. Well thought out and deliberately carried out attack plans now allowed the Japanese to overrun post after post with very little effort.

On the first of February, the Japanese began to surround Bagac. Two days later a company commander ordered an adjoining platoon to knock out two machinegun nests that had been spotted nearby. I volunteered to lead some of the men and advanced with the platoon. My commanding officer forwarded the following letter to General MacArthur following capture of the machinegun nests:

"For conspicuous gallantry and integrity above and beyond the call of duty in action with the enemy on 3 February 1942 near Bagac, Province of Bataan, Philippine Islands. When the rifle platoon of another company was ordered to wipe out two strong enemy machinegun nests 1st. Lieutenant Bianchi volunteered and of his own initiative, advanced with the platoon leading part of the men. When wounded early in the action by two bullets through the left hand, he did not stop for first aid but discarded his rifle and began firing his pistol. He located a machinegun nest and personally silenced it with grenades. When wounded a second time by two machinegun bullets through the chest muscles, 1st Lieutenant Bianchi climbed to the top of an abandoned American tank, manned its

antiaircraft gun, and fired into strongly held enemy positions until knocked completely off the tank by a third severe wound".

1st. Lt. Bill Bianchi was awarded the Congressional Medal of Honor for his heroic actions.

Chapter Five

1st. Lieutenant Paul T. George

I'm the last of the pub dwellers to share this tale. My name is 1st. Lieutenant Paul Theodore George, Jr. I was the mess officer at Fort Stoltenberg, Luzon, and along with Jack Kaster, who was a supply officer and Company Commander, was assigned to the 7th Materials Squadron. Jack and I sailed the high seas to the Philippine Islands aboard the same troop transport ship, the United States Army Transport, Republic.

If you'd be so kind, allow me to also take the time to fill in a few of the gaps in my upbringing so that you'll come to know me as well as the other guys. I promise not to drag this out.

From what I'm told my father was a bookbinder. When I was nine or ten he was drafted or volunteered for military service. Off he went to fight in the big war, and was promptly killed in action. As a result, I never got to know him.

My Mom, however, took the time to paint a picture of him I will never forget. There were numerous pictures of him all over the house, so I came to know what he looked like. Of course, the pictures became fewer and fewer over the years, especially when

Mom finally started dating again. She taught me how gentle he was and how caring and loving he was of her and me.

He was a good-looking guy with a chiseled chin, high cheek bones, a head full of wavy black hair and brown eyes. I suppose I loved him, but probably not like Bill Bianchi loved his father. Bill had many years of fond memories with him before he died, and that's different, I think. However, he was my Dad and I have a special place in my heart for him!

My Mom was a great Mom. She had a hell of a time for quite a few years after losing my Dad. Besides raising me and my brother, William, she managed a resort right outside San Diego. Eventually she married an OK guy in the late 1920s. A roofer, himself a widower with no kids, he was also a veteran of the war. By 1933 he was admitted to the National Home for Disabled Volunteer Soldiers in Santa Monica with active tuberculosis. After several years, he was discharged. By this time my Mom had died, I believe from a broken heart.

After high school, I went on to graduate from the University of California in 1937 with a BA in Psychology. Heaven only knows why I went for that degree. It's my belief that because of my Major in Psychology, and the fact that I served as the chairman of the complaint committee in my senior year, the Army decided my skin was thick enough to serve as a mess officer. I know I never volunteered for the job.

Anyway, like Jack, I didn't figure there'd be a call up so soon. In June of 1941, there we all were heading to the Philippines. As Doctor Swanson said, we did get our butts handed to us on Luzon from the very beginning. Strafing and bombings, day and night inflicted numerous casualties. When the Japanese began to invade with their main force of sixty thousand we escaped from all around Clark Field and hastened our retreat. Soon our first line of defense was being established on the peninsula.

As mess officer during this time my duties continued to be attempting to feed the men. It became more and more of an impossibility. When mules were killed during bombings, we had steak and hamburger for a few days. When we could catch a monkey or an iguana we had lunch. Men were literally starving to death.

By March, with the Japanese closing in, President Roosevelt ordered MacArthur to Australia, leaving General Jonathan Wainwright in command of all U.S. forces. Immediately, the Japanese tested the General's resolve beginning another wave of air and artillery attacks. By early April they brought in fresh reinforcements who renewed their attacks all over Bataan. They could break through any defense established by the allies. Exhausted now by continuous combat and weakened by starvation and disease, it became apparent our men could no longer defend themselves. General King, commander on Luzon, finally said, enough is enough. He surrendered on April 9th, 1942.

Chapter Six

Major Wendall Swanson, M.D.

The fighting on Corregidor in April of '42 was much the same as that on Luzon at the beginning of the war. The Japanese originally shelled the island constantly for about a month, sending in fresh troops after softening us up. Until then we had been handling the overflow of casualties from the main island. Now, with the addition of our own wounded, conditions proved to be somewhat overwhelming.

With the number of patients swelling tremendously everyone began working twelve hour shifts seven days a week. There were often days where we worked more than twenty-four hours in a row with few, if any, breaks.

♣♣♣♣♣♣

In the, "for what it's worth" category, we seldom treated Japanese soldiers, simply because their military doctrine forbade surrender. Their philosophy stated that if they raised the white flag and gave up they would be a disgrace in the eyes of their family and friends. The only acceptable outcome in such a situation was to continue fighting until they were killed in action or to commit suicide if they were captured.

With such rigid discipline and unwavering allegiance to their Emperor, Japanese soldiers believed that the enemy should be held to the same standards. With surrender being a punishable crime in the views of the military in Tokyo, as soon as a Japanese soldier captured an American they would impose immediate punishment, a firing squad with one target. Knowing this, Americans, in their attempt to avoid capture, would often fight to the death.

During my weeks and months in the tunnel, I would put into practice much of what I had been taught at Fitzsimmons. Called "meatball surgery", it meant keeping the patient on the operating room table for the shortest time possible while totally meeting their needs. It often meant debriding grenade fragments embedded in their soft tissue and muscles of their legs and arms, opening a patient's chest or belly if those same fragments or a bullet entered those cavities, or performing a tracheostomy if their airway was compromised.

Orthopedic surgeons were found performing amputations where necessary or splinting extremity fractures. At home, such broken bones would be repaired using plates and screws. In combat, the rule of thumb was to never further contaminate a wound by introducing yet another foreign body already contaminated by clothing, rusty metal or just plain dirt.

Because of the sheer number of cases, patients became either a "nephrectomy", a "debridement", or a "laparotomy". Later, making rounds on the nursing units, they became men with faces, families, friends and a name. Those moments helped us understand our purpose here. Subconsciously during surgery, this caring would most often be expressed in our surgical proficiency.

PART TWO

THE BATAAN
DEATH MARCH

Chapter Seven

1st. Lieutenant Jack Kaster

In late March and early April of 1942 there was a lull in the action. Many thought that the enemy was simply starving us out, which could easily have been the case.

Others disagreed, believing the commanders of such fierce and fearless fighters would never allow victory to be achieved in such a superficial manner. That notion soon proved to be correct.

Overwhelming air attacks began anew as did artillery and mortar barrages. Head on assaults by fresh reinforcements indicated that, true to their military tradition, these bastards were going for our jugulars.

On April 9th, word on Bataan and then Corregidor spread that General King had surrendered his troops on Luzon. Word had it that he had disobeyed direct orders from General Wainwright and MacArthur to mount a counterattack against the Japanese. It took guts for the old man to take the action he did. Aware that his men were severely dehydrated and malnourished, and crippled by the scourges of malaria, dysentery, beriberi, and diphtheria, he prevented what certainly would have been a slaughter had he not done so.

The day after the surrender found units across the island falling to pieces. Rifles, helmets, ammunition, and anything military littered the roads in all directions, especially on those leading to Corregidor. We were told to find our way promptly to Mariveles, a small town in the south of Bataan, to surrender as POWs. Many opted to take the risk of attempting to escape versus being captured by an enemy, who to this point, had fought an extremely cruel war. Many made it. Just as many became moving targets in their desperate attempts to outrun the Japanese.

With all this going on, it wasn't long before the fear of God crept into our very souls. It wasn't the fear of death that bothered us so much, but rather the real possibility of horrific torturing.

We began this ordeal with only the faintest ray of hope for humane treatment. Unlike the last promise made to us for "thousands of troops and hundreds of planes", every single one of us knew better.

En route, groups merged as twenty became fifty, fifty became a hundred. At Mariveles thousands became tens of thousands. The sheer numbers soon overwhelmed the Japanese. Certain the campaign to take the Philippines was going to take much longer, the Japanese thought that "the herd" would have been considerably thinned out. They were prepared for at the most twenty-five thousand prisoners. The seventy thousand Filipino and ten thousand American men now posed serious problems for the enemy.

The next day, to try to gain control of the situation, the Japanese began to assign four to six soldiers to act as guards for every one-hundred prisoners. Every fifteen minutes or so, a group was ordered to string itself out, streaming north toward the railhead of San Fernando, some sixty miles away. Here, we were told we'd board trains for half a day's ride to Capas, the nearest railroad junction to Camp O'Donnell. After another nine-mile march to the camp, only then would our journey end at an unfinished Filipino Army base built by the Americans. This base became our home away from home for what could possibly turn out to be years.

Our first day had barely begun. With several hundred men strung out in front of us, our captors took the time to show every one of us who was truly in charge. At the edge of a nearby jungle some four hundred NCOs and officers had been gathered. Without the blink of an eye the Japanese mowed them down with machine gun fire. Leadership capable of encouraging and planning escapes, either now or later—removed. Four hundred mouths to feed --- gone.

Meanwhile, each of us were being searched. Our possessions: money, rings and watches were confiscated. At the same time, anyone found with items such as yens was bayoneted on the spot. The assumption was that the man with yens had killed a Japanese soldier to acquire them.

Killing quickly became a regular occurrence. Men had their throats cut when riders in jeeps dangled bayonets from opened windows as they passed lines of marching men. Men were beheaded for any expression of displeasure, disemboweled for staring at a guard, shot for simply complaining about the heat. Collapsing soldiers were pushed from the ranks to the roadside by guards where "clean-up crews" would make certain they were dead.

Underway once again, having gone but a few miles, the heat exhaustion and dehydration began to show their effects. Men began to lag behind. Immediately they were shot, beheaded by soldiers wielding samurai swords from horseback, or run over by trucks carrying troops and supplies. Men stepping out of line to relieve themselves or dashing to one of the many artesian wells along the way were shot or beaten to death with rifle butts.

By days end we had passed the bodies of some one hundred Americans and over one thousand Filipinos. Except for two black eyes and bruises all over my body from a beating by the guards for no reason, I could thank God, I was still alive. I had survived day one of the "Bataan Death March". Many of my friends had not survived, and many more would soon join them.

A POW is beheaded by a Japanese soldier using a shinto gunyo sword - a sight all too common on the Bataan Death March.

Day one of the Bataan Death March.

CHAPTER EIGHT

1ST. LIEUTENANT PAUL GEORGE

On day two of the march I spotted Jack Kaster with a few of his men two or three groups ahead of us. A close friend who had served all these years in the same squadron, I felt badly when I noticed he was toward the back of the pack struggling to keep up.

I found out that Jack was slightly wounded on the first day of bombardment of Clark Field. He was then wounded a second time, but much more seriously. An exploding mortar sprayed hundreds of red hot fragments into both of his legs. Now, badly scarred and in constant pain from some irretrievable pieces of shrapnel and the muscle and nerve damage to his lower limbs, the Japanese began to take advantage of his misfortune.

Occasionally, a guard would run into the mix of men. With all his might, he would kick or club one or both of Jack's legs instantly bringing his body crashing to the ground. Men around him who instinctively jumped to assist him back to his feet were they themselves beaten severely with a rifle butt.

Day three and four were no better than the first two with abuse starting at the crack of dawn, not stopping until after nightfall. A guard practicing beheading a man told us that the "art" of beheading was to have the body slump to the ground while his head bounced several feet away. Guards tempted men with a sip of muddy water from the roadside puddles that would cause dysentery. Badly dehydrated, many accepted. Those who refused were given thirty lashes with a bamboo switch.

The most horrific event I witnessed on the march occurred when a man was bayoneted in the chest for falling behind. The gasping sound that came from the soldier tore the soul from my body. I will never forget it!

Darkness did have one major benefit: the torture stopped. Our captors who had walked the same ten or twelve miles, needed sleep as badly as did we.

Shortly after dusk each evening a group of about five hundred of us were gathered closely together, directed off the road, and herded to the center of a field. Here we were ordered to lie down and settle in for the night. If it was raining that, was our problem. If it was cold, that, too, was of no concern to the Japanese.

A dozen guards became one, who, while the others slept, walked leisurely around the perimeter of our sleeping and tightly huddled horde.

Not unforeseen, without a hint of moonlight visible, as soon as the guard had passed our small section of men, three or four Philippine soldiers would crawl off into the surrounding darkness and begin their journey home. With the Philippine Army in ruins the Japanese assumed these men would never fight against them again. Therefore, they turned a blind eye toward their escapes. They assumed, with as many as one hundred Philippine soldiers escaping each night, it would help to "thin the herd", reducing their responsibilities for the remainder of the march and in the POW camps.

Americans, on the other hand, had no place to go. With a $50 bounty on the head of each of us, we knew we'd never find a place to rest our head on Luzon. Most of us were only able to dream of home. There were duties at night, important "duties" performed by both American and Filipino soldiers. All came with considerable risk of detection and retaliation. None were taken lightly.

The first duty was for men to collect two, perhaps three, canteens that the Japanese had not yet confiscated and somehow were hidden on their person. (More than three would tend to rattle, alerting the guards to what was under way). Once the guard had passed, the soldiers with the canteens would begin a one hundred-yard crawl to the nearest artesian well. Here they'd hold the canteens under water, fill them and return. Quickly they were passed around, each man taking a small sip until the canteens were empty, and another trip was begun to the wells. With many men making many trips, most men had at least a few thirst quenching sips each night.

The other duty each evening, just as dangerous, was for men to slither on their bellies in the opposite direction – toward the road. With bloated bodies littering the street gutters and the incredible stench repulsing even the staunchest individual, men traveled from one dead soldier to another removing anything beneficial to the living. Pith helmets or floppy cotton hats were a God send for men who had lost theirs during the surrender and whose bare heads were now blistering from the unbelievably strong April sun.

Tremendous caution was required regardless of how often or in which direction the men headed. A crackle or a clunk in the distance often alerted a guard. He would fire three or four shots into the spot where he thought he had heard the noise. Frequently, we heard a moan from a soldier he had wounded or killed.

Prisoners caught stealing water or robbing dead bodies were tortured and killed. A common practice by many guards was to stake the man naked, spread eagle to four posts in the ground. There they would be left baking in the sun as we began our march in the morning. I always thought that had to be a horrible way to die.

On the fifth day, we finally were fed a small ball of dirty rice. We complained about neither the size nor the quality. This was the only time on the march we were given food. We were never offered water. I'm certain the Japanese knew about the canteen runs at night and withheld water specifically for that reason. Those canteen runs and occasional sips of water from ditches along the way, that almost certainly caused dysentery, saved a lot of lives.

A much needed break on the Bataan Death March.

GIs carry their sick or injured comrades on the Bataan Death March.

Chapter Nine

1st. Lieutenant Bill Bianchi

It took us a total of six days to go those sixty miles from Mariveles to the railhead at San Fernando. It was nearly a week of witnessing the most barbaric and inhumane treatment one individual could possibly inflict on another. On the last day, killing seemed to have become an overwhelming obsession with the Japanese. Many more prisoners, perhaps one hundred Americans and a thousand Filipinos, lie on the side of the road. Most had been shot in the head or bayoneted in the chest or back. In some places bodies were stacked two or three high. I never realized human beings could be so cruel!

In the railyard outside of town, sat several antiquated steam locomotives and coal tenders. Hooked to each other were a half dozen World War 1 four feet by eight feet wooden boxcars used to transport cattle. Each held eight animals. Somehow the Japanese managed to squeeze one hundred men into each car. Packed in so tightly it was impossible to sit or lie down, and very difficult to even breathe. With the floor covered in manure, becoming more slippery from men relieving themselves, keeping our footing was a big challenge. The heat, humidity, and the thousands of flies all added to our already long list of woes.

I was about three rows back when the door finally opened. The rush of air felt as if I had an oxygen mask on. It had to be at least twenty degrees cooler outside of the car. Many of us thought that anywhere had to be a hell of a lot better than where we were. Yeah, right!

The trip had taken about five hours. I really don't remember much, as I slept most of the way standing up. Suddenly, as we were disembarking the train, we watched two of our men, now without support of any type, slump dead on the floor. They could have been dead for hours. The mass of humanity had kept them upright. It wasn't unexpected, I suppose.   Nevertheless, it was very disheartening.

Now that we were among people who did not yet know us personally, we thought, just perhaps, we might get a break from our constant misery. That was not to be! As soon as our feet hit the ground the beatings and stabbings began once again. It was as if we were watching a rerun of a horror movie we had seen only yesterday. We still had a dreadful nine miles to Camp O'Donnell. We set out at a record pace. Again, we thought, or hoped, anything had to be better what we had just endured.

Chapter Ten

Major Wendall Swanson, M.D.

We learned quickly of the surrender on Luzon and received daily reports from guerillas as to the brutality being handed out by the Japanese. Things looked as dismal from inside the Malinta Tunnels as I'm certain they had to be on Bataan.

Within twenty-four hours the hostilities ceased on the main island. The Japanese big guns, however, then turned and took aim at our five square miles of paradise. It appeared from the very beginning as if the enemy was trying to wipe us off the face of the earth.

Most of our casualties came from men defending the beaches where amphibious landings were taking place. Civilians were also being bombed. In addition to casualties, refugees filled the tunnels well beyond capacity. Life as we knew it on Corregidor was quickly slipping away.

The first few days following the surrender on Luzon, the sheer number of shells dropped on Corregidor would have awakened the dead! They were dropped constantly, day and night, aimed at our remaining gun emplacements and defensive beach trenches. Japanese observation balloons floating high above the island gave clear views of each. As a result, the enemy could fire howitzers with high angle trajectories right into deep ravines on the beaches and directly onto our gun emplacements.

Within a few weeks, the island was a barren rock with guns silenced and beach protectors destroyed. Troop numbers were drastically reduced. Towards the end of the month, some twelve thousand rounds of combined air and artillery shells a day were falling on the island. Morale among the men was taking a very heavy toll. There were several reports of soldiers committing suicide by placing the barrel of their 1903 Springfield or English Enfield beneath their chins and pulling the trigger.

Early in May, the Japanese attempted to land some two thousand soldiers along the North Point Beach. Men of the 4th Marines killed or wounded twelve-hundred of the enemy before they ever reached land. The remaining eight hundred Japanese, however, raised havoc killing or wounding our few remaining defenders.

On May 6th, the Americans sent some five hundred reserves against eight hundred and eighty fresh Japanese reinforcements landing on Corregidor. The numbers dictated that any skirmishes between the Americans and Japanese were easily won by the enemy.

Mid-morning on that same day three Japanese tanks made it on shore and began heading toward the Malinta Tunnels. Realizing that the defenses outside the tunnels could no longer defend what was inside, Lieutenant General Wainwright seriously considered accepting defeat. Fearful of the fate of the one thousand wounded and hundreds of staff inside, he decided that the few hours of freedom that might be gained by standing and fighting were probably not worth the sacrifice of hundreds of lives that would surely be lost if he did not surrender. In a radio message to President Roosevelt, Wainwright stated that there was a limit to human endurance. That point, he said, had certainly been passed by his men. With that announcement, two officers were assigned to carry a white flag to the Japanese.

Life inside the tunnels became unbearable between the surrender on Luzon and that on Corregidor. The constant bombardment had eaten away any sense of sanity. The supply of water dwindled and food became impossible to find.

I was in the operating room on the 6th when the announcement was made over the hospital loud speakers that General Wainwright had surrendered all Allied forces in the Philippines. We heard that doing so came only after the implied threat of the firing of shells directly into the main branch of the Malinta Tunnel as well as the slaughter of remining forces on Corregidor. The General had no other choice.

The Japanese allowed us to complete the surgeries we were performing during the announcement and on patients awaiting surgery at the time. We were permitted to perform surgery all the next day, as well as to care for the one thousand men filling beds on the hospital wings.

Over the next few days, the enemy began to clear the tunnels, first by sending refugees home and by sending ambulatory civilian Filipino patients along with them. Meanwhile, hospital staff, unnecessary for direct patient care and ambulatory Filipino and American soldiers, were sent several miles outside the tunnels to a place known as the "Garage Area". Here, next to a barely recognizable garage leveled by shellfire, sat a concrete slab, (perhaps a parking lot) one hundred and fifty feet wide by fifteen hundred feet long. Surrounded by barbed wire this area now became the mustering point for all prisoners from the tunnels as well as those captured from around the rest of the island.

Each man had a number painted on the back of his shirt or pants as he entered the holding area. All were warned that if they wandered beyond the wire without a guard they would be shot. As I recall there was not a morsel of food nor a drop of water for the first three days. What there was thereafter did little to prevent the fifty to sixty deaths that occurred each day.

Suddenly, like a slap in the face, we were fiercely introduced to the true nature of our keepers. Guards walked among the thousands of prisoners taunting them by pouring the contents of other prisoner's canteens on the ground in front of any man begging for a sip of water to quench his thirst. They would whip, kick, or punch men if they blocked their way, often for no reason at all. They would bayonet Filipinos and Americans alike for grumbling about having no shelter, the lack of medicine, the hot sun, or a hundred other complaints. Day and night, standing or attempting to sleep while lying on the concrete slab without being stomped to death, the brutality was non-stop.

For the next two or three weeks as men died they were placed on a blanket, the four corners tied to a bamboo pole. Two POWs with the pole on their shoulders, would carry each man about two miles to a mass burial site. Here, in trenches dug by enemy bulldozers, the men were laid fifty to a row. One of the two dog tags from each man was removed. These were given to an officer in camp assigned the duty of compiling lists of men who had died and were buried in the Philippines. The remaining dog tag was left on the body, possibly to aid in identifying the soldier's remains after the war.

Often the men carrying the dead would they themselves collapse and die from disease or starvation. They, too, would be carried the remaining distance and placed in the trenches. Occasionally, men carrying the dead would collapse from exhaustion, still alive and breathing. They also would be carried to the trenches, and buried alive for no other reason than some Japanese private with a rifle gave the order to do so.

Finally, on May 24th, with patients from the Malinta Tunnel Hospital who could walk being forced to join them, prisoners from the Garage Area were walked to nearby docks, and loaded into the holds of three transport ships. Crowded in so tightly all were forced to stand. Evening turned into night, the long night into morning. With no one allowed topside to relieve themselves and no bathrooms available, the rusty iron floors were soon covered with the human waste of prisoners no longer able to hold their bladders or suffering from dysentery. Had we not become used to such treatment it would have seemed inhumane!

With high tide in the morning, all three ships hoisted anchor, and sailed off in what was a northerly direction. Several hours later, about twenty-five miles across Manila Bay, all three ships arrived at a small port just south of Manila.

Immediately, with their spiteful and vicious behavior, guards began beating prisoners with clubs to hasten their departure from the ships. Quickly assembled into columns of four, this filthy ragged mass of humanity was paraded through the streets of Manila.

After five miles, we were told we were heading for a city jail now a temporary POW camp known as the Old Bilibid Prison. We were informed that here we would remain for only as long as it would take the Japanese to finish readying several POW camps across the Philippines. It was estimated the task would take another two weeks.

The trek through town served two useful purposes. First, it demonstrated to the Filipino people the superiority of the Japanese over the Americans. More importantly, as we sauntered down Dewey Boulevard in the center of Manila, four abreast, curb to curb, block after block of the grungiest looking soldiers you can imagine, our eyes were drawn toward the old University Club on our left. To our utter amazement, on the front porch stood a red-eyed General Wainwright, head down, his shoulders shrugging repeatedly as if he was crying uncontrollably. Behind him stood his senior staff. It suddenly became obvious that while we were being forced to "pass in review", officers were here to first hand shoulder the guilt for the misery on those marching in front of them. The "Gloat March" as it is known today, served the Japanese purpose well – for the moment.

Once the men spotted Wainwright the slouching vanished. Backs straightened, all began to "left, right, left, right" marching in step so familiar to military order. As each group approached the General its leading man would emphatically bellow, "Eyes, left"! In unison, all heads snapped forty-five degrees to the left affording each man the ability to look directly at the General. The lead man, himself facing the General, saluted, symbolically doing so for each man in the group. "Eyes, forward", brought heads back straight ahead, and the march continued. These were stirring moments!

We felt sorry for the "Old Man". As we neared the prison our concerns, however, returned to the reality of our status as POWs. Guards resumed beating men. Guys at the tail end of the line were shot for simply lagging behind. One man was shot for breaking ranks and attempting to drink water from a puddle at the side of the road. In addition, we witnessed a beheading because a soldier had cursed a guard.

PART THREE
POW
and
INTERNMENT
CAMPS

1942-1945

Chapter Eleven

The Santo Tomas Internment

Camp in Manila

Within the centuries old walls of the original city of Manila sits the Santo Tomas University, named in memory of the Dominican Theologian, Saint Thomas Aquinas. The primary purpose of the University was to prepare young men for the priesthood. Still run by Dominican Fathers at the beginning of the war, its many buildings and numerous classrooms, along with forty-eight acres were taken over by the Japanese. All would soon be converted into an internment camp for allied civilians and military nurses.

Within days of its takeover, the enemy had collected thousands of American and British men, women, and children, and imprisoned them within the now fenced in compound. Poles, Dutch, Mexicans along with one hundred U.S. Army and Navy nurses, eventually became part of this very crowded communal camp.

Prisoners were given sleeping quarters in one of the plentiful classrooms. Each room became a dormitory. Hundreds of men jammed into the gym, women and children were placed into each room in the main building, and teenage boys squeezed into rooms on the third floor of the Education Building. Some eighty infants and their mothers were housed at the Holy Ghost Convent. The Convent provided extra care for the babies and help for the moms.

A piece of cardboard, when found, was used as a "sheet" between a prisoner and the wooden or concrete floor. Rooms were so crowded that counters in labs, gym benches, and permanent upright seats in lecture halls served as beds. Toilet facilities for twelve hundred men in the Main Building consisted of thirteen toilets and twelve showers. Indeed, lines were long. Over time, some six hundred men constructed additional showers and toilets. They also worked on improving cooking facilities and setting up bath tubs as hair washing stations. It was a constant struggle to control flies and mosquitos.

With the Japanese deeming self-governance should be the rule of the day at Santo Tomas, an Executive Committee was formed. The Committee managed an astounding twenty-seven departments, including their own police force and sanitation department. Initially, they allowed internees to visit with Filipino prisoners and other inhabitants of neutral countries for a few hours each morning at the front gate or along the chain link fence. Here, the "haves" with money in local banks and friends willing to help them spend it, could buy groceries, have their clothes laundered, and have newspapers delivered. The "have-nots", meanwhile, survived with only the clothes on their backs, and received what little food the "haves" might contribute for the first few days. After that, the Japanese put in place the logistics to begin to feed the entire camp.

Visiting privileges were soon abolished because the Japanese felt a rich-poor attitude was developing among the prisoners. Simultaneously, the openings in the fence and gate were covered with bamboo mats to conceal activity from the general population. After three male prisoners escaped, they felt they were losing control, and began to crack down.

Monitors for each room were assigned. A 7:30 P.M. curfew was initiated. Roll call was performed by monitors every night. "Lights-out" was at 10:00 P.M. The three escapees were recaptured. In front of the Chairman of the Executive Committee and the monitor, they were tied to a pole, tortured and executed.

At Santo Tomas, other than this execution, the Japanese were surprisingly neither cruel nor abusive. If control was maintained they became most lenient. Perhaps the best example of their tolerance was allowing the internees to build huts called "shanties" and plant vegetable gardens in the campus courtyards. When completed, prisoners could escape the mass of humanity in the classrooms, and retreat to the quiet of their shanty during the day. They were still obligated to return to their room each evening for the 7:30 curfew and nightly roll call. When the University became severely overcrowded, the Japanese allowed four hundred families to live in their shanties around the clock.

Another example of their change of heart was the effort they took to feed the POWs. Although there was no food for the "have-nots" while the compound was being established, a committee was quickly formed. Each day a few could leave camp to make food purchases from the locals. Funds provided by the Philippine Red Cross were issued to provide at least two nutritious meals daily for the entire population of the camp. Breakfast consisted of cereal, bread, and coffee. The second meal of the day was served in the late afternoon. It included a stew with meat, sweet potatoes, vegetables and, of course, rice.

Life during the last few years at Santo Tomas, although unsettled, was not all bad. There were sports programs including soccer, basketball, and a baseball league with its own World Series. There was a baptism, a mock high school graduation, and even a barn dance for teenagers.

The hospital, situated in an old engineering building, was adequately staffed with doctors and nurses to care for a continuous population of up to one hundred and fifty outpatients a day. Patients requiring surgery or intensive care were sent to hospitals in Manila.

Things began to unravel in early 1943 when the increasing population caused the POWs to become agitated. To relieve the tension, eight hundred men were placed on trains and transferred some thirty-five miles to a new camp at the University of the Philippines at Los Banos. With the number of POWs doubling and doubling again, systems within the camps soon reached their breaking point.

Civilian   administrators   were   replaced   with   Japanese Commandants.   They ordered all committees be dissolved. Without guidance sanitation declined rapidly.   With no police force crime skyrocketed.   When a supply officer replaced the food committee, only a small portion of the money that was previously allocated for meals was provided with a predictable decline in the quality and quantity of the food.

On November 14th,1943 a typhoon ravaged the island of Luzon. Most of the shanties at Santo Tomas were washed away beneath twenty-seven of rain.   What little food the internees had squirreled away was lost also lost in the storm. Most of the crops on the island were wiped out. What little survived the storm such as coconuts, became very expensive.

A few weeks after the typhoon, attempting to avert disaster, the Japanese gave each prisoner the one and only Red Cross package they would receive during the entire war.   Adults and children alike were presented with a staggering forty-eight-pound box of canned beef and other meats, cheese, chocolate, cookies, candy, cigarettes, vitamin, quinine, and, so on.   The timing of this early Christmas present could not have been better.   It staved off serious malnutrition for the time being.

By March of 1944 the Americans were knocking on the door of the Philippine Islands. With the situation deteriorating in the South Pacific, many Japanese who had never been directly involved in the war effort, now saw an opportunity to do so.

Commandants cut prisoners rations to fifteen hundred calories a day, then to eleven hundred calories a day, and finally to seven hundred calories a day. This insured that many prisoners would surely die of starvation.

By the end of the year, treatment at Santo Tomas had become much harsher. If there was an air raid, which happened frequently, the next meal would be withheld. By then the Japanese were substituting lugao, a tasteless rice with the consistency of oatmeal, in place of meat stew. Broken sinks, toilets and showers went unrepaired. Bathrooms became cesspools. Waiting lines grew longer and longer. With not a bar of soap to be found, body lice on clothing and blankets became commonplace. The camp was filthy, rat infested, and crawling with cockroaches.

Some POWs lost over 30% of their body weight. This made it impossible to exert enough energy to even tend the gardens, which had supplied additional food. For the first time at Santo Tomas, deaths were attributed to starvation. Burial details were a sight few had ever thought possible. They now occurred daily.

From a radio hidden in camp POWs knew of American progress island hopping their way towards Luzon. Hopes were high a rescue would be imminent. As January dragged on, the number of prisoners dying from starvation climbed to twelve a day. In one of their final attempts to be as vengeful and as cruel as possible, falling short of actual beatings or torture, the Japanese began to substitute an unusual fish soup for lugao. With the guards openly cooking and eating fish in the main dining tent, the heads and tails from their tasty repast were dropped into pots of water and left for the prisoners to prepare as their one and only daily meal.

One day, four camp leaders were dragged away and executed for having contact with guerilla forces in the area. Rumors circulated of a possible massacre of all Japanese military and civilian prisoners. Fear oozed from every crack in the compound.

Finally, on February 3rd, 1945 five American tanks came crashing through the entire front fence at the University. What should have been the happiest day in over three years was marred when the Japanese guards took over two hundred POWs as hostages. They demanded that they be set free in exchange for the prisoners. Eventually, all the guards were released. Now Santo Tomas POWs were fed, received medical treatment, and began preparations to return home.

The Navy Nurses were transferred to Los Banos to establish a hospital there. The sixty-four U.S. Army Nurses had the honor of being the first Americans to exit Santo Tomas for the states. None of the nurses had died during their confinement.

"Dugout Doug", meanwhile, had returned to the Philippines. With his usual flare, he showed up at Santo Tomas on February 7th to take credit for the rescue. With the war still going on, the Japanese acknowledged MacArthur's ego, promptly shelling the campus, killing twenty-eight, including sixteen POWs.

Other POWs began evacuations by boat or plane beginning on February 22nd. Seven people had been executed by the Japanese. In total four hundred and fifty died of starvation, forty-eight that month, the highest death total for any month since the camp had been opened. Approximately three thousand, eight hundred prisoners were released from the camp. Manila lay in ruins beyond the walls of Santo Tomas.

Santo Tomas University Education Building shanties occupying parking lots & rows of vegetables filling the front lawm.

Chapter Twelve

Lt. Jack Kaster
At Camp O'Donnell

Just prior to the start of the war, Camp O'Donnell was under construction by the U.S. Corps of Engineers just outside Manila. It would become part of the Philippine Army's 71st Infantry Division. With the outbreak of the hostilities, however, the unit was sent north to fight the Japanese. Within weeks they were retreating to the Bataan Peninsula. Here, along with seventy thousand other troops they were forced to surrender.

A week later the first of sixty thousand Americans and Filipino POWs began arriving at Camp O'Donnell. This was the ending point of the Bataan Death March. Somewhere along the sixty plus mile journey some twelve thousand men had simply disappeared. A majority of that number, perhaps ten or eleven thousand, were Filipino. While it is true that a few thousand had escaped into the jungle, most had been brutally slaughtered by the Japanese. They were beheaded, died of heat exhaustion, run over by a truck, shot or even hung. If you can think of a method of execution, the Japanese had undoubtedly used it.

The 71st had lost many good men in battles on Luzon, and many more on the Death March to Camp O'Donnell. Those numbers continued to climb. An additional two thousand Americans and twelve thousand Filipinos died at the camp during the first eight weeks it was open.

It was calculated that if deaths continued to occur at that pace all the POWs at the camp would be dead by the end of the year. Concerned about being accused of genocide in the eyes of the rest of the world, the Japanese evacuated the American prisoners to another camp where the death rate was much lower. The camp sat about a hundred miles north of Manila, about four miles west of the town of Cabanatuan, from which it took its name. Camp O'Donnell was cleaned up and turned into a rehabilitation center for Filipino prisoners. When they were all pardoned and released about six months later, the camp was closed.

Lt. Paul George and I arrived at Camp O'Donnell within hours of each other on its opening day in April of 1942. We left together when it closed its gates to Americans in June of the same year. We feel, each as strongly as the other, that there's a story to be told here. Why did so many young men die in such a short time? Understanding it all is not the least bit difficult.

To begin, let's go back to the surrender on April 9th, 1942. We had been beaten, and badly beaten. We were forced to drop our weapons and raise our hands, not to a numerically superior force, but to a host of tropical diseases unknown to the rest of the world.

At that time, we were all severely dehydrated and on the verge of death. Most of us were close to point of starvation, and so dehydrated we were unable to sweat. We were then forced to begin the Bataan Death March. Here we were one week later, alive…. but barely.

At the same time, we can't forget that the Japanese drove MacArthur from his home in the Philippines. They defeated some of the best-known generals in the world on the battlefield. Yes, they succeeded in binging tens of thousands of Americans and Filipino fighters to their knees.

Regardless of the circumstances, Japan held her thumb of power over all she had conquered. She had no intention of easing that pressure anytime soon. At the gates of Camp O'Donnell, the Japanese were making the rules and enforcing them with an iron fist.

Lists with hundreds of rules were posted at the entrance and prominently throughout the camp. Violation of any came with consequences. The punishment correlated with the severity of the infraction. A minor infraction, such as arguing with a fellow prisoner, would result in standing in the sun holding a fifty-pound rock above your head for several hours. Attempting to escape, a major infraction, would result in being tied, standing with your back against a post in the center of the camp for two days, finally being used for bayonet practice.

Though not every punishment was as severe, most were meant to humiliate the man, bringing him much closer to his breaking point. One such rule was having EVERY prisoner salute ALL Japanese soldiers and officers. Neglecting to do so resulted in the Japanese immediately selecting several American officers at random. The chosen American officers were then obligated to punch the offender in the face until he fell unconscious to the ground. Not doing so with enough power netted the officers doing the punching a rifle butt in the back.

Raising your voice to a guard landed you in solitary confinement, being denied a meal, sometimes two, or even three. Kneeling on a two by four board without a hat, shirt or pants in the midday sun for an indeterminate period became a favorite disciplinary action for a multitude of sins, including eating another man's meal when he was unable to do so, or complaining about the taste of that very meal.

Speaking of meals, there was only one each day consisting of rice and native sweet potato made into a thin, watery gruel.

Occasionally, pieces of fish would be added. These tidbits almost always came with a few maggots floating in the bowl.

Even more of a detriment than the starvation diet was an insufficient water supply. Three spigots located in the center of the camp ran day and night. There were very few canteens, cups or even coconut shells to hold the water. A man standing in line for ten hours for his turn at the tap would think twice about sharing. Dehydration quickly became the number one killer at Camp O'Donnell.

With fifty deaths a day, burial details were a necessity. They were organized and efficiently managed by the Japanese. Each evening some two hundred of the healthiest men felt likely to survive the task would be selected. Their names were posted on a bulletin board. They were required to report to the hospital the following morning regardless of weather conditions. Every fourth man was to pick up one of the bamboo stretchers standing outside.

With the body count increasing and the morning air becoming increasingly foul, groups of four prisoners, including the man with the stretcher, were quickly chosen and assigned to work together. Each team respectfully placed a body on the stretcher, covered them with a blanket, and headed off to the cemetery, about a mile and a half from camp. Two armed guards accompanied each team.

Upon arrival at the cemetery they set their charges aside. As was the custom, one dog tag was removed and returned to the senior officer in camp, the other dog tag was left on the soldier.

The first four men were given shovels by the guards and promptly set about digging a grave twelve by twelve by four feet deep. Each grave would eventually hold fifteen men.

The second four men arriving at the cemetery would begin to place bodies into the grave. Men following were tasked with holding down the bodies with sticks because they were now floating to the surface in ground water seeping into the grave, aided by gas from decomposition of the bodies. The first four men who had arrived would then fill in the gravesite with dirt.

Burying fifty men a day created not only a tremendous physical toll on our bodies, but a colossal emotional load on our minds as well. Just witnessing men dying in such numbers produced a tremendous drain.

With no quinine to prevent or treat malaria, even men who never had it, contracted it. Men with the disease quickly progress from one phase to the next. A good percentage of those men died. Combined with other diseases, they never stood a chance.

Malaria was characterized by recurring bouts of high fever alternating with teeth chattering chills, each phase lasting three to four days. At night, lying next to or near a man with chills was cause for shattered nerves. Constantly through the night he would scream and beg for more blankets to be tossed on top of the six already covering him.

Likewise, we'd lose a full night's sleep in the barracks with a man who was crying in pain as he was going through the fever phase of the disease. With a temperature of one hundred and five, drenched in sweat, these soldiers sometimes attempted to peel the top layer of skin from their bodies with their fingernails.

Beriberi, caused by lack of Vitamin B-1 in the diet, was another killer. "Dry" beriberi, which I initially suffered from during my brief stay at Camp O'Donnell, effected sensation in both my arms and legs resulting eventually in loss of mobility. When I could walk, I did so with a distinct gait called the "beriberi shuffle". Eventually I became completely paralyzed from the waist down. The paralysis lasted for almost a year.

When my "dry" beriberi disease turned to the "wet" type it attacked my cardiovascular system. I became short of breath with the least bit of exertion. My legs swelled to twice their normal size. My heart raced constantly. I often became confused as to where and who I was. Many men died of this disease, primarily from congestive heart failure. Miraculously, somehow, I survived.

♣♣♣♣♣♣

The causes of most of the deaths, pure and simple, were lack of water, starvation, cruelty and outright neglect. While the Death March itself killed tens of thousands, more importantly, it set the stage for many more to die within a matter of weeks or months.

One contributing factor that reduced the number of mouths to feed was the "No work—No food" policy. As a result, men fought fiercely among themselves to volunteer for work outside the prison. Building roadways and repairing runways quickly burned up more calories than the one thousand provided in gruel each day. Few could keep up. On our worst day two hundred and fifty men lost their lives.

The fact that the camp was a pig sty also contributed to the high death rates. With soak pits for urination dotting the landscape and slit trenches for defecating dug everywhere, the twenty-seven-acre site became a virtual sewer. Minor scrapes became infected, and with no medications to treat them, they often led to lethal results.

All the men were filthy. Water from the spigots and the river were reserved for drinking only. Bathing came solely from very infrequent rain showers. What little clothing we did have was not only dirty but torn and tattered. A few men resorted to wearing a loin cloth provided by the Japanese.

In addition, while some four hundred of us slept back to back in a barracks built to hold one hundred, there were just as many who had no shelter whatsoever. With little shade, exposure to blistering sun all day, and few willing to share water, men became dehydrated quickly and succumbed to organ failure.

Our few months at Camp O'Donnell could not have ended soon enough. With conditions worsening, and the degree and number of atrocities on the rise, a glimmer of optimism arose with the rumor of us transferring to Camp Cabanatuan. Thus far we had witnessed an enemy with an incomprehensible hatred. We assumed and prayed we had seen the worst of the worst. Why we thought things would be different elsewhere I have no idea. Regardless, all we had left was hope!

Camp O'Donnell Mass Grave

Chapter Thirteen

Major Swanson
at the
Old Bilibid Prison Camp

I was ill prepared for Bilibid. Remember, I'm a doctor, not a fighter. I was being forced to face an ordeal for which I could have never imagined.

"Intimidating" was my first thought as I attempted to count the many guards atop the massive stone walls surrounding the prison. Armed to the teeth, six men paced between guard houses spaced about every sixty yards. Inside each guard house were two more guards, each manning a machine gun. One faced inside towards the heart of the prison, the other toward the perimeter outside walls.

The gawking eyes of the guards, rifles cradled in their arms and grenades clipped to their belts, combined with the deadly implications of the automatic weapons, clearly conveyed the message that indeed you may enter these premises, but there's a good chance you will never leave here alive.

Hustled through one of the three sets of heavy metal gates into the prison we were immediately greeted by about a dozen American prisoners. Captured by the Japanese from all over Luzon during the weeks just before the surrender on Bataan and Corregidor, they were but a few of the several hundred Americans scattered throughout Bilibid. Following handshakes, hugs and a few tears upon recognizing old friends, we were broken into groups of fifty men and taken on a quick "tour" of the camp.

We learned that Bilibid was built in the 1860's in the same shape as an old wagon wheel. The "hub" of the wheel, a large circular building, was now quarters for the prison guards and office space for administration. Eleven long one story wooden structures, the "spokes" of the wheel, served as barracks for prisoners and the thousands of newly arrived critically ill Americans. The high, thick, stone walls formed the "rim" of the wheel.

The barracks were simply dilapidated frameworks. There were openings for windows, but there were none. There were several doorways, but no doors. The leaky old roof was but a means for rain to enter and gather in puddles on the concrete floors. Mold was rampant on the ceilings and what little wall space there was.

One building served as a hospital. Unlike the other barracks, it had wooden bunks with straw mattresses. The bedding quickly became saturated with excrement of patients with dysentery. Their bodies were covered with bottleflies. Within days of our arrival the hospital filled to over flowing. All too soon, men began to die.

A few days into our stay, two corpsmen and I were working in the hospital when two Japanese soldiers entered, approached us and gave us thousands of quinine tablets to hand out to our patients. We treated all the men with active disease including the most critically ill, but lacked sufficient supply to treat the remainder of the camp. Still, the drugs were most appreciated.

Entering the barracks, we had the opportunity to chit chat with a few of the leaders who had been the earliest POWs at the camp. Curiosity among both groups led to a volley of questions. "When is

MacArthur returning"? "Do our families even know we're alive"? "Why no real brutality or cruelty from the guards".

First, as far as we knew MacArthur was not returning any time soon.

Second, since we knew that the Japanese had not notified either the Swiss government nor the American Red Cross, as to who was at Bilibid, we were certain our government had told our families only that we were missing in action. What our families would conclude was anybody's guess. Lastly, a myriad of factors contributed to the lack of cruelty displayed at Bilibid as opposed to elsewhere, and the biggest reason was probably the Commandant.

The Commandant of Bilibid was given the responsibility of maintaining order among the civilians throughout the surrounding city of Manila. With most of his small administrative staff and many of his prison guards needed to aid in restoring electricity, rebuilding the police department, and sweeping the streets of rubble, the leader was required to use every ounce of his imagination to get the job done.

Ultimately, the challenge of meeting the expectations of his supervisors, while overseeing the care of over two thousand POWs, came with a simple solution.   The Commandant asked the Americans to remain at Bilibid for the duration of the war.   He explained that the Americans would be most helpful processing prisoners on their way to camps outside the Philippines. There they would work in copper, coal mines or other industries in Japan or Manchuria.

In addition, the Japanese officer presented the men with the possibility of taking over complete administration of the camp. A second unexpected request. Duties would include purchasing food from local merchants, preparing and rationing them, disciplining prisoners, and assigning and transporting men to and from details in Manila. The list of duties seemed to go on forever.

He promised that he would try to increase rations and improve medical care. He did caution the men, however, that by himself, he had little control of such matters. Nonetheless, after having heard rumors about other Commandant's attitudes and their approval of atrocities against prisoners at other camps, the men agreed that working together would be beneficial to all involved. Handshakes all around sealed the deal.

Two days before our departure to Cabanatuan we were eye witnesses to an example of "clearing house" for which Bilibid would become known. Four hundred technicians, specialists in radio repair and weapons manufacturing, along with hospital laboratory technicians, arrived for transfer, we assumed, to Japan. A list of names, ranks and occupations was prepared for the ships manifest, but for reasons unknown, no other records were ever kept.

Within hours another group of Americans arrived, this time a mere two dozen. Labeled as hardened criminals by the Commandant at Camp O'Donnell, more for their attitude than anything, these men found themselves shackled one to the other. They were now on their way to the Davao Penal Colony on Mindanao Island far to the south of Luzon. Here, they were sentenced to five years' hard labor in a camp where brutal mistreatment was commonplace and survival rates were dismally poor. No other records other than the ship's manifest was ever kept of these transfers either.

On the day we left Bilibad, I believed I would get to see many of these men again, perhaps returning home from the war, maybe in Hawaii being issued new uniforms, or getting together again disembarking from our homeward bound ship in San Francisco harbor. Somehow, somewhere, we would meet again.

American barracks at Old Bilibid Prison.

Chapter Fourteen

Major Swanson
At
Camp Cabanatuan

On June 3rd,1942 after just nine days at Bilibid, five hundred men and I were packed into boxcars for the four-hour ride to the recently opened Camp Cabanatuan. It didn't take long for us to realize that as POW camps go, Bilibid had not been that bad. I'd lost a few pounds and was covered with lice, but I had never been horsewhipped or beaten with a golf club. Fleas and bedbugs that embedded my blanket at Bilibid left me with many infected bites, but while there I had never seen men bayoneted for stealing food or beheaded for raising their voice to a guard.

On that very same day there were nine thousand other prisoners in boxcars, trucks or on foot marching from all over Luzon to one of the three camps at Cabanatuan. Men from Camp O'Donnell, Bilibid Prison, and hospitals on Corregidor and Bataan were evenly distributed among what were simply called Camp One, Camp Two, and Camp Three.

The camps were four, eight, and fourteen miles to the west of the city. Totaling a combined area of one hundred acres, each was surrounded by an eight-foot-high, three strand barbed wire fence attached to neatly trimmed tree trunks sunk deep into the jungle floor.

Being the first to arrive, the seven thousand men from Corregidor and Bilibid trudged to the furthest camp from town, Camp Three. We did this so as not to clog the narrow dirt road between the camps.

Though Camp Three had several water towers and siphon pumps meant to draw water up to the storage tanks, they had either been stolen or shattered beyond repair.

After the Japanese squeezed six thousand Corregidor men into Camp Three, they reluctantly marched the overflow of one thousand men next door to Camp Two. It wasn't until they arrived that they realized there was absolutely no water within the camp – no wells, no storage tanks, no siphon pumps, nothing! The only source of water was a well one thousand yards outside the front gate. This required a bucket be lowered to the bottom, with a two hundred-foot rope for retrieval. The following morning, the same one thousand prisoners were paraded over to Camp One. Its functional wells and equipment were placed on line, and the water towers filled.

Men continued to arrive. Over the next several days prisoners were moved around so that only Filipino troops remained in Camp Three. Water trucks delivered water daily, but soldiers were only allowed to fill one canteen per day. Seldom was there enough water to accomplish this task. Healthy men became ill, the sick got sicker. In July, there were seven hundred and eighty-six deaths in Camp Three from dehydration.

Camp Three had become merely a holding pen for Filipino troops to keep them from returning to the battlefield. After three months of dealing with horrific conditions the Japanese considered them "rehabilitated". Those that had survived were pardoned and released. The camp was closed in September of 1942.

Naval personnel, who seemed healthier than soldiers on the battlefield, along with the healthier Americans were placed in Camp Two. The logic was they could make more frequent trips to outside the wire to perform the manual task of lowering and hoisting a full water bucket. This did relieve the burden on the troops placed in Camp One and Three.

Directly across the road from Camp One sat a recently built, unused hospital compound. Consisting of thirty wood framed shacks, each had enough upper and lower bunks constructed of wood slats with flimsy mattresses to hold forty patients.

With over four hundred medical personnel scattered throughout the three camps, we requested permission to use the compound as it was intended. Without medications or surgical instruments, while we would be unable to treat the diseases or conditions afflicting the men, it did still make sense to isolate the sickest and terminally ill men from the relatively healthy population.

Within a week, we received approval to open the hospital. We fenced off ten of the thirty wards to quarantine the most severe dysentery. We assigned around the clock physicians and staff and filled twelve hundred beds with twenty-five hundred patients.

By the beginning of December, the number of deaths at Cabanatuan steadily began to decline. I wish I could say it was the result of some magic elixir we dispensed at the hospital, but it was, in all honesty, simply due to the change from the rainy season to the dry season. Small and slow running creeks around the edges of the jungle and puddles all over the island began to dry up. The breeding areas for mosquitos and flies disappeared.

Our patient load remained at over two thousand men a day. There, too, were reasons for this. While the number of malaria and dysentery patients declined, many more men were now admitted to the hospital with other terminal diseases. Having been POWs for eight, nine or ten months with nutritionally deficient diets, signs and symptoms of conditions known as pellagra, scurvy, etc. began to appear. All these diseases progressed rapidly, and led to blindness, mental instability, gangrene of the toes, and agonizing deaths. Unable to treat these patients without medications, we kept them as clean and comfortable as possible. A staff member remained with every one of them as they passed away.

♣♣♣♣♣♣

An awful lot happened during the fall of 1942. In addition to my duties at the hospital, I was assigned to work the wood chopping and camp farm details. While on these details I met, and became very good friends with Jack Kaster and Paul George. Young Lieutenants, both were skilled leaders of their men. More importantly, they possessed the ability to empathize with the pain experienced by those around them, and the compassion to share that misery. To see these men sharing two or three capfuls of water or a few tablespoonsful of soup or rice might seem insignificant, but were tremendous sacrifices and meaningful examples.

The wood chopping detail was made up of six hundred of the healthiest and strongest men working seven days a week. Teams of two took turns felling trees so as not to exhaust any man too quickly. Wrapping strips of torn loin cloths, provided by the Japanese, around our hands prevented blisters from forming until calluses could develop.

Common practice was to fell trees from the fringe of the forest at the base of the Sierra Madras mountains. We worked our way inward so as not to be hidden from the guards, and to remain as close to the trucks hauling the wood as possible. The straightest of trees were used as fence posts at the prison camp. They were cut into twelve or fourteen-foot lengths, branches removed, and bark stripped. All other trees were cut into cordwood before being placed on the trucks. The wood was delivered to the Commandant's quarters and to the mess halls. Since no fires were allowed in the barracks, no wood was allotted for prisoners.

A farm created by the Japanese, which eventually expanded to over five hundred acres, employed over two thousand prisoners a day. Groups of one hundred men were assigned to hoe, plant, harvest, and carry water for irrigation. We used the same loin cloths to protect our hands as we did for chopping wood. A variety of fruits and vegetables were planted and, upon maturation, picked and distributed, primarily among the Japanese soldiers, either for their personnel use or to sell to Filipinos on the black market.

Occasionally, Paul George would successfully request that the enemy mess officer allow us to have the left-over crops after they were harvested and distributed. Welcomed treats such as an ear of sweet corn, juicy tomatoes, sweet potatoes to share, and onions for soups were thoroughly enjoyed by all.

A big morale booster came when we were informed we would be paid for our labor. Yes, paid! Privates were paid five centavos a day for labor, sergeants ten, and officers fifteen centavos. Converted to U.S. dollars, that equaled three to nine cents a day.

Work was verified on a time card carried by the prisoner and initialed by the guards at the work site. Cards were then tallied for half the camp every two weeks. The account was submitted and maintained at the camp canteen, the only place in camp where we could spend our earnings.

For sale at the "Mom and Pop" type store run by Filipino women were individual cigarettes, small bars of soap, cans of pork and beans, and peanuts in the shell for fifty centavos a cup. Since few men at the time did not smoke, cigarettes quickly turned into "money" at Cabanatuan.

Days became weeks, weeks turned into months. There were good days and bad, more often bad. Together, we faced the horrific conditions in this God forsaken place with the hope it would all soon end. In the meantime, all we could do was pray that maybe, just maybe, yet another "Hell" would soon be over!

Japanese military & American POW "Script" used during WWII.

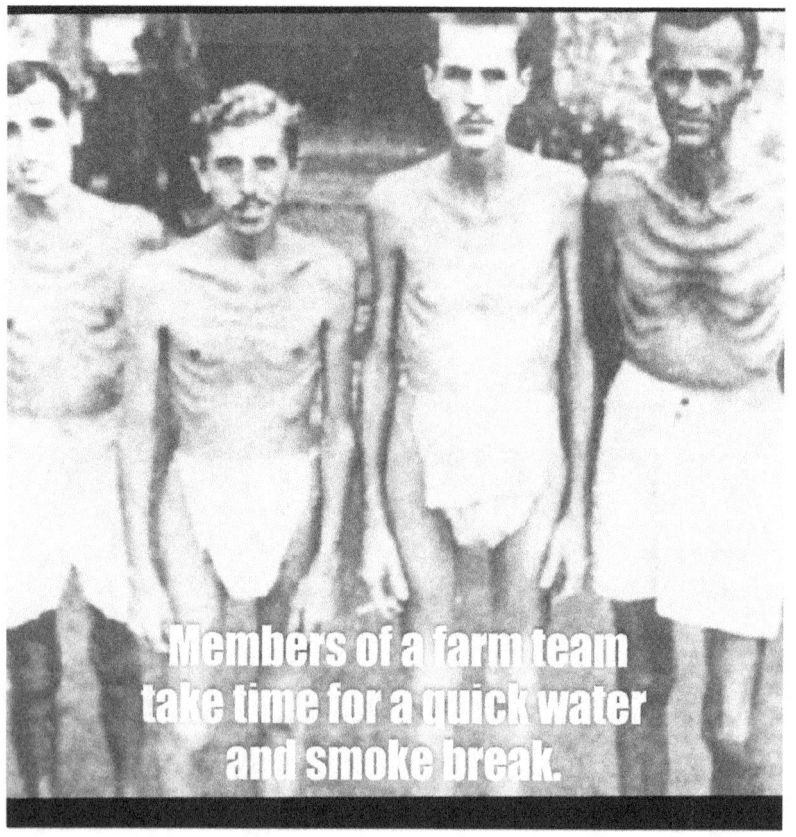

Members of a farm team take time for a quick water and smoke break.

Chapter Fifteen

Lieutenant Jack Kaster
At
Camp Cabanatuan

Sometime during our first summer at Cabanatuan, Paul George and I started to believe we'd be home by Christmas. The following year we had the same idea and again, the year after that.

Needless to say, we had suffered through many dashed dreams. Over the years there were also a few "up" moments. In the fall of 1942 Red Cross packages arrived. The Japanese elected to hold them until Christmas. It had nothing to do with a "Merry" holiday. Rather, it gave the Japanese time to pilfer the contents. The vitamins and medications listed on the packing slips were long gone. The food stuffs, however, including corned beef, canned vegetables, coffee and cocoa, helped to hold the death rates down for several months. All were desperately needed and enjoyed tremendously.

While the goodies were most appreciated, nutritionally they were a little too late for me. I was experiencing the late stages of "wet" beriberi. Paralyzed below the waist, I laid flat on my back at the hospital for almost a year. Thankfully, Doctor Swanson, who was a good friend, and others, made sure I was turned on my side and my stomach frequently. As a result, I never developed pressure sores on my back, buttocks, or the bottom of my feet.

The care packages nipped many deaths that would have been caused by malnutrition in the bud. In addition, the Japanese began to introduce pieces of carabao, dried fish, and mango beans into what had been up 'til then, strictly a rice diet. All had a positive effect upon us both physically and mentally.

Recreational items also arrived in the care packages. These included playing cards, cribbage boards, baseballs and bats, volleyballs and volleyball nets. Many men, as you might expect, were unable to compete in the physical games, having been weakened by either malnutrition or crippling beatings. Just as many, locked in deep depression, were unable to divert their minds from the feelings of hopelessness, and made no effort to participate.

There were, however, several intervals when even those in brittle states pulled themselves up and joined in whatever level of activity they were able. Remarkably, the motivation paid off. Overall morale increased across the camp for the duration of the war.

High morale gave rise to more planned escapes. Rarely were they successful. Consequences of attempting to escape were severe. Article fifty-eight of the camp rules read "the penalty for attempting riot, and attempted or actual escapes, will be death by firing squad".

Several escapes were attempted in 1943. All were thwarted. The first occurred when two prisoners were recaptured, tortured, and executed. The second when four men were recaptured, made to dig their own graves, then shot and decapitated, as the main body of prisoners were forced to look on.

Serious about preventing any further escape attempts, the Japanese extended the hours of the wood chopping detail to eighteen a day, and at the same time reduced the number of water breaks. The goal was to fell and debark enough tall trees to erect a second fence, some twenty feet from the first. Both were restrung with ten strands of wire a foot apart. Guard houses were built between the fences, with guards stationed every fifty feet, twenty-four hours a day. A new electrical system was installed to provide lights at night along the perimeter.

Notice was given to the POWs that for every man that attempted to or managed to escape, ten would be executed. Immediately, each man was assigned to a group of ten. Each was told to keep an eye on their fellow prisoners, especially at night.

Despite all the precautions taken, another escape was attempted, but also nipped in the bud. Eighteen men from two groups that had housed the two escapees were lined up along the fence and executed by firing squad in the presence of as many prisoners as the Japanese could muster.

The American Camp Commander, Colonel Leo Paquet, forbade any further escape attempts for several months. Eventually, he gave the green light and two men escaped. Though they were recaptured and executed, firing squads were never used again. Rather, now the punishment was to reduce rations for the entire camp for several weeks. Eventually, a few more men managed to escape. The jungle surrounding the camp did not make escapes easy.

With all the commotion going on about escapes, executions, and the like, guards grew angry. The brutality across the camp increased even more. Whipping with riding crops or switches became a common practice. The frequency of abuse doubled. No longer were your chances of being hit every day rare. Rather, they were quite probable. Guards were now grabbing shovels from men digging trenches or soak pits, who were, in their opinion, moving too slowly, and beating them across their backs and thighs, leaving massive bruises and open wounds. Because of the nature of the material on the shovels, most wounds became infected.

At the same time, supervisors on the camp farm detail issued a short wooden club to be used to keep the prisoners in check. Injuries skyrocketed. Many men were carried back to the barracks or to the hospital following a shift.

Again, days turned into weeks, weeks into months. Months ran on and on ....too many to keep track. The occasional ear of corn, fresh tomato or a Red Cross package never seemed to make up for the agony endured by every man, every single day. The goal of the Japanese was to break the will of every man. They were doing just that. All we could do was to try to endure whatever brutality the Japanese continually brought upon us.

Chapter Sixteen

Lieutenant Paul George
At
Camp Cabanatuan

If Camp Cabanatuan were ranked from one to ten as a pig sty, it would probably get a ten plus. "Filthy" and "overcrowded"; these two words most adequately described the conditions we endured at Cabanatuan.

True, there was a war going on, and this was a POW camp. One would never expect five-star accommodations with a famous chef preparing three, five course meals a day. No one would ever think that the treatment would be this inhumane. Or would they?

Barracks were built on poles or stilts, elevating the building some four feet off the ground. This was done to allow the monsoon rains to flow beneath them rather than through them. Unfortunately, many were built on slopes with the floor at one end of the barracks, well below the four feet elevation required. As a result, the plan ultimately failed.

During the rainy season, the Americans tried to reduce the problem by digging drainage ditches around the barracks. Without Japanese assistance to provide materials to hold back the dirt, the walls of the trenches simply collapsed, allowing water to flood most of the barracks.

With low lying latrines and soak pits, waste mixed with flood water and ran through each of the barracks. Not only did the flood water rot and ravage the wood, but then, as the water receded, waste would adhere to the flooring and walls causing an unbelievable stench. This situation attracted thousands of flies which spread dysentery and mosquitos which spread malaria.

The barracks were fifty feet long by fifteen feet wide. Built to hold forty men comfortably, with the massive influx of prisoners, each eventually housed over one hundred. There was no electricity.

With flooding and massive overcrowding, the buildings quickly fell into a state of disrepair. Bamboo walls and cogon grass roofs broke down. Living conditions became even more intolerable.

After several years, realizing that we might be there for several more, men salvaged materials from collapsing buildings, to repair those still standing. There was no relief from the overcrowding. With the excess lumber and bamboo, we fashioned doors where there were none and repaired holes in the walls and roofs as best we could.

We ate in mess halls, each serving several barracks that surrounded them. They were simply four, eight-foot high posts with the traditional cogon grass roofs. Inside sat several picnic benches at which to sit, and three or four iron caldrons hanging above shallow fire pits for cooking. Stacked fire wood sat nearby.

The hospital was just as crowded as the barracks. Each of the thirty wards meant to hold a maximum of thirty patients, now housed a minimum of ninety.

The dysentery area was quarantined. Its own wire fence surrounded ten wards. Within this area sat the infamous "zero" ward. Not counted when the wards were being numbered, it held the terminally ill men who had no chance of leaving the ward alive.

There was no pharmacy; we had no meds to stock it. There was an operating room, but no instruments or sterilizers. We had occasional dressings for wounds, but these were rare.

An act of brutality I will never forget. Two prisoners, caught taking food from locals through the outside fence, had their hands and arms tied together. Facing each other they were dangled from a cross beam erected in the courtyard. With their toes barely touching the ground, each received one hundred lashes. Here, they were left hanging overnight.

The following morning an American physician was called to apply dressings to the numerous raw slashes to the men's faces, arms, chests, and backs. When the doctor left the scene, the men were again flogged, this time until they became unconscious. Dressings and dirt from the whips were now embedded into their bleeding wounds. The men were simply left to die. It took two days for them to do so. These were the most horrible and excruciating deaths I ever witnessed!

It became obvious in the early months of the war that if the Japanese were not able to house triple the number of prisoners they expected to capture, they would be unable and unwilling to feed them. That is exactly what happened.

Rice, the mainstay of the Japanese diet, became ours as well. Theirs was supplemented with meat and vegetables. We were given mango beans, the tops of native sweet potatoes, and a few small pieces of fried fish. On average, we were fed only one thousand calories a day--- a starvation diet for men performing manual labor.

Constant cravings drove us to take chances whenever and wherever we could to steal food. The problem was that getting caught eating crops while harvesting, bribing guards, stealing from the mess halls, or dealing on the black market with Filipinos or other prisoners, were all cause for reduced rations for weeks.

Calorie counts varied from week to week depending on the status of the war. A good week for Americans in the field would stir a need for vengeance on the part of the Japanese. The result was an immediate increase in brutality and a decrease in rations.

With retaliation by the enemy, we continued to take potentially lethal chances while at the same time looking for alternatives to fill our bellies. Unfortunately, stray dogs and cats, iguanas, and snakes roaming the camp became acceptable food sources. We were desperate. At the same time, I am proud to say, our resident mascot bulldog, "Soochow", survived!

♣♣♣♣♣♣

From the moment the camp opened until the day it closed, there were two "black markets" running at Cabanatuan. Bringing in medicine, mail, and money had the same primary goal; plainly, to provide food for all of us.

Of all the men in camp, only one percent made it through the front gates with money or valuables in their possession. Somehow, whether it be in their underwear, in their hair, or between their toes, these men made it past the many Japanese searches.

The one system flourished for about six months until the "chief operators" were caught and executed. Despite the tremendous amount of illegal and immoral money transactions a few of us won our fight against starvation due to their efforts.

The second "black market" was much better organized. It operated for almost two years. In the summer of 1942, two American women, whose husbands had died at the camp, began the underground system. They themselves had somehow avoided internment at Santo Tomas.

Working hard with merchants and farmers, Margaret Utinsky, known as "Miss U", and Claire Philips, "High Pockets", started shipping food, medicine, mail, and money, all known as "baked cookies", to a Filipino woman, Evangeline Neibert, or to Sassie Suzie", from Manila to the marketplace in the town of Cabanatuan.

Here, the "cookies" were received by Naomi Florres, known as "Looter", a Filipino vegetable vendor. She, in turn, would break the merchandise down into small lots, hide them in the center of sacks of rice, and deliver them to the camp.

Nearing the end of their road, the sacks were delivered to Lt. Co. Harold Johnson, and infantry officer in charge of the Cabanatuan commissary. The goods inside the sacks were removed and distributed to six officers designated as "helpers", who, as the last cog in the wheel, delivered the goods to the men who had placed and paid for the orders.

In May of 1944, several men in Manila were found to be involved in the operation. They were briefly imprisoned but soon executed. "Miss U" and "High Pockets" were also captured, imprisoned for several months, and then released. With the entire operation exposed by the Japanese, it was terminated.

Some things never changed at Cabanatuan, like the lice and fleas infesting our clothes and blankets. Delousing and DDT powder reduced their numbers. Sleeping even became more comfortable for a while. The comfort never lasted, however, because those little insects were always quick to return.

Clothing and boots were a constant problem. With no replacements available constant wear and tear destroyed them in short order. Most of us opted for the loin cloth offered by the Japanese and went barefoot. Others would strip dead comrades of boots, shirts and pants. Others cut material from their clothing for patches. There always seemed to be a needle and thread available that had somehow been smuggled into camp.

Little things made a big difference during our stay while at Cabanatuan. For example, we named the trails running through the prison. Market Street and Broadway ran parallel, both crossing Second and Third Streets. There was even a Buboltz Boulevard, a path leading to the latrines, named by and after a man from Milwaukee, WI.

Sending home postcards provided by the Japanese began in November of 1942. This was a small but tremendously appreciated privilege, allowed four or five times a year thereafter. The message could contain a mere twenty-five words informing the family of where the camp was, our general state of health, and a small personal message. Return mail was not allowed until 1944. In the meantime, families were at least made aware of our status. This privilege kept us sane.

With the collapse of the underground in May of 1944, as they say, "The wheels began to come off the cart". Reprisals began swiftly when the Commandant drastically reduced rations. Brutality became constant again and even more extreme. The Japanese did almost nothing to maintain sanitation. Conditions quickly became deplorable!

By August, word had spread that Japan was uneasy about the prospect of losing her main source of forced labor if the United States recovered the Philippine Islands. With all due haste, authorities in the homeland requested that the thousands of POWs be transported from Cabanatuan to Japan, Taiwan, or Formosa. Here, we would work in coal mines, steel companies, aircraft manufacturing, and construction sites.

A few weeks before the rumors about transferring began, Dr. Swanson met and became good friends with 1st Lt. Bill Bianchi from a small town in Minnesota. Assigned to the Philippine Scouts he, too, was among the many captured on Bataan, and forced to make the Death March. Dr. Swanson watched as the young Lieutenant pleaded with the guards to get extra food for hospitalized patients. He did this often and often succeeded.

Sitting around a picnic table one morning, Dr. Swanson, Jack and I were having breakfast. with the Lt. Col. who ran Will's outfit. While eating we heard the tale as to why Bill had been put in for the nation's highest honor, the Congressional Medal of Honor. Seems he went on an excursion to search and destroy a few machinegun nests with a rifle company that adjoined his. The leader of that company asked him to lead a few of their men. It was just his day to take a few bullets for the "Gipper". Apparently, he's the kind of guy that doesn't let much stop him from achieving his goals, and it was only after being wounded three different times and taking out two machinegun nests, that he finally quit for the day. A truly remarkable guy!

A few days later, Will, Dr. Swanson, Jack and I were gathered at the very same picnic table playing cards. It was a Sunday, declared by the Japanese as a day of rest. Our discussion focused on the chances of any of us being relocated. Our guess was that if half the population of the camp was leaving, being healthy and able to work, we would be a part of that group. Our view was that things were getting so ugly at Cabanatuan it might be better for us to move on. Thus far, we'd gone from one Hell to another Hell. Now we feared that could certainly happen again. We decided we really had no control over anything. It was time to leave everything in the hands of God.

Claire Phillips
Known as "High Pockets"
Spy & Smuggler at Camp Cabanatuan

Chapter Seventeen

Doctor Swanson
Returns to
The Old Bilibid Prison

It had been almost three years since my first terrifying "visit" to Bilibid. I must admit my return trip in September of 1944 was just as bad. Jack, Paul, Will, and I had won the "lottery", so to speak, at Cabanatuan. As a result, we became part of a group, mostly officers, on our way, first to the "clearing house" at Bilibid, and then to God only knew where.

Not surprisingly, the American staff who had been at Bilibid the first time around were still there. They helped reduce our anxiety levels tremendously. Sitting at long tables, clipboards in front of them, pencils at the ready, the staff informed us that they could keep us together if we all signed aboard on same ship heading to, of all places, Japan. Eager to complete this journey together we all signed on.

The ship to Japan was to take us to Nagoya on the South Central Pacific side of the island. From there we would be transported to the Mitsubishi heavy industrial plant, and quartered in military barracks. Here, we would work six to seven days a week. We were told we would be working on the manufacture of railway equipment, tanks, and the world famous "Zero" combat aircraft.

With the Americans now bombing Manila from the air around the clock, it was impossible for the Japanese to bring transport ships into Manila Bay.   Still, POW camps, adhering to schedules previously established by the Imperial Japanese Navy, continued to send prisoners to Bilibid.

Because of the one thousand prisoners arriving daily, with no ships sailing, conditions deteriorated rapidly.   Rice, once again, became a rare commodity.   Water was unavailable for days at a time.   Men slept where they fell.   The stench of feces and urine was unbearable.   It was Camp O'Donnell and Cabanatuan combined. We prayed for ships to arrive soon.   Finally, bombing raids over Manila slowed.   All types of Japanese passenger and cargo ships once again began to creep back into the harbor.

On the 12th of December, after three months of waiting, a roster of one thousand six hundred and nineteen, mostly officers, of which the four of us were a part, was read aloud.   We were told to gather our goods and say our goodbyes, expecting to be loaded aboard the ship the following day for transport to Japan.   We went to sleep that night not knowing if this was a reprieve from the "Hell" of Cabanatuan or simply a step into another, perhaps an even worse one!

Part Four

The
"Hell Ships"

Tale of the
"Oryoku Maru"

Chapter Eighteen

Boarding the "Oryoku Maru"
As Told By
1st. Lieutenant Bill Bianchi

It didn't take long to figure out exactly how horrible this trip was going to be! Trouble was, we didn't want to believe it. We'd heard rumors from several sources around camp; the Japanese who had been guards on sunken ships, and the Americans who had survived a sinking, were rescued by the Japanese, and returned to Bilibid. We all wanted desperately to believe they were stretching the truth, just a bit. Hoping for the best, we agreed that whatever we had heard about the "Hell Ships" was greatly exaggerated. We decided to take what we heard with a grain of salt.

Unaware at the time that it was simply a dress rehearsal, at dawn on December 13th, 1944, the sixteen-hundreds of us marched several miles from Bilibid Prison to Pier Seven in Manila. Here, we gazed upon a sleek looking passenger ship, three tiers of luxurious cabins atop her deck. Her name, "Oryoku Maru", showed faintly through a fresh coat of rust colored paint on her bow.

No sooner had we begun to debate who would occupy the cabins, when we saw thousands of Japanese soldiers and hundreds of horses being unloaded from the ship. The stench of the horse manure reeking from the holds took our breath away! Like thousands of ants, the Japanese came streaming from the cabins, briskly dropping down from one upper deck to the next, reaching the main deck. From here they spread out descending one of three very steep, very shaky wooden stairs heading to the dock below.

Once the Japanese determined that they could get us to Manila in an orderly manner, we returned to Bilibid to await the next high tide scheduled for that evening.

Arriving back at camp, we were met by the Commandant standing atop several empty ammo boxes inside the main gate. In his usual charming and pleasant manner (just kidding), he informed us that the "Oryoku Maru" had received her sailing orders. We would return and board at dusk. Soon after that we would get under way for the city of Yawata on an island at the Southern tip of Japan. We would be housed at the Fukuoka Number Three Branch Camp. We would be working for the Nippon Steel Company, six days a week. We were promised no mistreatment. We would receive adequate water, and would be well fed. Yeah, right! Hadn't we heard all this before?

We were also told that the "Oryoku Maru" was an extremely fast ship, able to maintain nineteen to twenty knots per hour. Translated, that meant, even with a zig-zag pattern to avoid submarines, we would reach Japan in as little as five days.

At dusk, we said our goodbyes for a second time, gathered our belongings, and made our way back toward Pier Seven. Once there, we were broken into groups of eight hundred field grade officers, five hundred junior officers, and three hundred enlisted. Each group was instructed as they boarded that they were to climb a specific set of stairs. Once we had reached the deck further instructions would follow.

After several hours of waiting to board, a group of about two thousand Japanese men, women, and children passed us by. All proceeded along the pier, and began to board the ship. Rather than stopping on the main deck, they climbed to cabins on the upper decks and filled them well beyond capacity. All opportunity for a chance to relax in the atmosphere of a beautiful ship's cabin was now completely dashed!

At dusk, word was passed quickly to begin boarding. Three lines formed. It took us only minutes to reach the top. Junior grade officers took the stairs leading to the foredeck, enlisted men went to the middeck, and field grade went to the afterdeck.

All three columns of men proceeded to the center of the ship, where we encountered open hatches into which we were forced to enter. Prodded by bayonets to speed up our descent, we, for fear of falling into what we could only see as total darkness, cautiously crept down steeply slanting, rickety staircases, six decks down to the very bottom of the ship. Here, we were forced to the furthest recesses of the hold, crowded onto wooden platforms built ten feet out from the hull, with only three feet high between them. We could neither stand nor stoop. We were forced to sit with our knees against our chests, against the back of the man in front of us. By now, "Hell Ship" was embedded into the minds of every single man on board.

Chapter Nineteen

On Board the "Oryoku Maru" As Recalled By Lieutenant Paul George

By nightfall there was total darkness inside the ship. Not a speck of light reflected off the hand in front of your face, the hull so near your head, the hatch so many decks above.

With the only air supply now covered with a heavy iron hatch cover, things went from bad to worse very quickly. As men became "air hungry", they gasped for relief. The first death of the night occurred when an officer, suffering from asthma, went into respiratory arrest. The Japanese ignored the entire event.

Shortly thereafter, buckets of a sloppy rice mixture, along with "Honey Buckets", were lowered into all three hulls. Not able to see which was which, we often dipped our hands into the wrong bucket giving rise to some goodhearted laughter. Like the buckets themselves, it was too little, too late.

With the temperatures in the holds rising rapidly to one hundred and thirty degrees, dehydration quickly occurred. Men began screaming for water.

Because the screams disturbed the Japanese passengers, the guards covered all three hatches. Now without almost no air, men began to suffocate in the deepest corners of the holds. By morning our numbers had decreased by at least fifty.

Urine and excrement covered the entire bottom of the hull. The platform boards dripped down through the cracks onto men sitting below who were unable to move. The stench of horse manure combined with human waste was beyond nauseating. Conditions were beyond unbearable!

In each hold, no matter what rank, men died of thirst, wallowing in filth, and steeped in hopelessness. Some began demonstrating weird behavior. Men with knives crawled over dead bodies in the darkness, stabbing those below them and drinking their blood. Others drank their own urine.

Eventually, exhaustion ruled. All became eerily quiet. What we had hoped for was nowhere in sight. What was to come, we did not know. One thing was certain, things could only get better, couldn't they?

Chapter Twenty

Underway on the "Oryoku Maru"
As Recanted by Major Swanson

At the crack of dawn, the next morning, the guards removed the hatch covers. With a little light and air getting in we began the grueling task of removing the men who had died in the three holds. Among the dead I helped carry topside that day were Major Houston B. Houser, Adjutant to General Wainwright, and Major James Bradley, of the famous Fourth Marines. With the steps to the deck too narrow to accommodate more than two men carrying one body, it took hours to remove all the dead. When they reached the deck, a chaplain said a few words. Each man was then simply pushed over board. This, I suppose, was the Japanese ritual for a burial at sea. For several hours, we used the cover of darkness to maneuver north through the narrow channel between the Bataan Peninsula and Corregidor. Transporting bodies topside allowed us to observe the passing terrain. We all agreed it had to be the now deserted Subic Bay.

While there were no longer any military for the Japanese to fear as we passed the once mighty American Naval base, we suddenly realized that our ship was unmarked. Not even a Red Cross, which the Allies would never attack, was on her stack!

Escorted by four smaller ships flying the Japanese flag, we became prime targets for torpedoes and bombs from American submarines and carrier based planes closing in on the Philippines. Now, not only did we have to worry about the Japanese trying to kill us, but also friendly fire possibly doing the same.

Having completed the burial detail breathing became a bit easier. We calmed down a bit after the Japanese promised food, water and fresh "honey buckets". Unfortunately, we could never tell which bucket was which! All of those lowered from above were just bent and beaten old five-gallon gasoline cans.

Chapter Twenty-One

Underway on the "Oryoku Maru"
As Recalled By
Lieutenant Jack Kaster

The lugao breakfast was actually pretty good! It was pasty, as usual, but the rice was peppered with a few bits of fish and seaweed. Tea was provided for drinking.

Without warning the buckets were suddenly hauled up to the deck, the hatch covers suddenly thrown back on. Firing began from several anti-aircraft guns overhead. We were told it was just a routine air raid drill. We knew better!

All at once we heard the whine of dive-bombers, exploding bombs, and bullets splattering the outside hull of the ship. Men anxiously scurried to the top of the stairs to peek through cracks beneath the hatches, and report the action to those below.

Wave after wave of American dive-bombers, we assumed from the USS Hornet, dove at the ship, dropping their bombs as they peeled off. They returned again and again strafing us with machine gun fire. Judging from the cheers on deck, at least two of our planes had been knocked out of the sky.

That day, although not one bomb struck the "Oryoku Maru", five hundred Japanese nationals traveling in the top cabins were killed by machine gun fire. Many more were injured, including a dozen Americans below deck. The superstructure of the ship was severely damaged.

Once the planes returned to the carrier, the "Oryoku Maru" limped into Subic Bay and dropped anchor. Here, in the dead of the night, wounded Japanese were removed, the dead left on board.

As the activities of that day ceased, we attempted to survive in the "sewer", which was becoming filthier by the minute. Empty "honey buckets" no longer arrived. Full ones used all day in the total darkness were used again, and again, and again. The amount of human waste in the bottom of the ship became deeper, and deeper, and deeper. It was almost more than we could bear.

Breathing once more became a problem in the deepest corners of the holds, most difficult for field grades in the after hold. Having been designed as a baggage room, there was absolutely no ventilation in that hold. Each breath taken decreased the oxygen by that amount. As a result, seventy men suffocated that night.

With breathable air becoming less available in all the holds, we were all in various states of mental confusion. Fighting, knifings, and other bizarre behavior resulted in several more deaths. Any man who tried to escape through the hatches was immediately shot by the guards.

In the middle of the night, the Japanese abandoned ship, leaving only a few crewmen, gun crews, and guards to watch the hatches. They told us we would be transferred to land the next morning. Suddenly, we hoisted anchor, sailed one thousand yards away from the mainland and dropped anchor again. We were now a sitting duck for the planes that would surely return to finish the job.

The American planes did indeed return about 8:30 the next morning. At least a dozen waves of six aircraft each came in low, at first circling the ship. Eventually they gained altitude, lined up the ship, and began diving straight down, making their bombing runs.

The remaining Japanese scurried to abandon ship, releasing prisoners in the holds below by removing hatches. Weak from malnutrition and befuddled from the lack of air, we were all extremely slow ascending the stairs.

Within minutes the aircraft made two direct hits. The first hit was atop the after hold. Many field grade officers were killed or wounded. The second hit was on a lifeboat just leaving the ship carrying six Americans wounded the day before, along with six Japanese. All were killed.

Chapter Twenty-Two

Sinking of the "Oryoku Maru"
As Revealed By
1ˢᵗ. Lt. Bill Bianchi

As the bombs started dropping, all hell broke loose. The Japanese removed the hatch covers, shouted that we were to remove our shoes, exit the holds, and abandon ship.

Men emerged from the first two holds rather quickly. Many were covered with a light dusting of rust fragments broken from the inside of the hull with a bomb blast. Jack Kaster had been injured from falling metal, but he managed to move out with us. None of the other men from our hold appeared injured.

The men from the rear hold were much slower getting off the ship. Many were bleeding profusely, dragging badly wounded and dead comrades behind them, choking on the thick black smoke now belching from the hatch.

Paul and I helped Jack make it up the stairs to the deck. The three of us ran like hell, leaped as far as possible from the ship, and plummeted into the ocean below. On the way down, another prisoner halfheartedly joking said, "It was time to do the laundry anyway"! The jokester made an unbelievably frightening moment less traumatic.

As we swam to shore, we heard men left on deck screaming that dozens of men were still alive in the rear hold. With flames blazing from the hatch, the stairs had burned to ashes. No one dared to reenter.

Several hundred yards away from the "Oryoku Maru", we gazed back at what we imagined would be a gruesome sight. To our amazement, the flight leader of the first wave had made eye contact with some of the men in the water. Gently, he rocked his wings back and forth, a signal to us and to the other pilots. He had recognized those in the water as Americans, not Japanese soldiers. Swooping across the bowel of the ship, wave after wave of aircraft gained altitude as they headed east. Our relief was indescribable!

Despite the reprieve, many men unable to swim, drowned. Men from the rear hold with serious wounds were also lost. Guards, both on the ship and on the beach, began shooting men straying from the main group of prisoners swimming ashore. The shooting went on for hours.

Later that day we headed towards two fence enclosed tennis courts about a quarter mile up the beach. Suddenly, the same aircraft that attacked the ship earlier that morning reappeared. Following a fly-over to confirm the ship had indeed been abandoned, the rearmed and reenergized pilots took careful aim on the "Oryoku Maru". Two bombs struck the forward hold hitting ammunition magazines. One explosion after another literally blew the ship to pieces. By late afternoon, the "Hell Ship" laid at the bottom of Subic Bay.

Chapter Twenty-Three

Farewell Major Swanson
As told by
1st. Lt. Paul George

With all the excitement having ceased, the Japanese ordered us to form groups of fifty for a head count. When the second count agreed with the first of one thousand, three hundred and forty-nine we entered the tennis court through a gate at one corner. They assigned us spaces of twenty-six rows of fifty-two each. We could sit, stand or lie down, but were forbidden from roaming around, other than going to the latrine or getting a drink of water. There were straddle trenches several feet outside the gate, and a lone spigot just outside the same entrance.

In the same corner seventeen seriously injured men were segregated. They received minimal medical care. Doctor Swanson was among them. Word reached us that he was very badly injured. Extremely concerned for him, we approached as a group to express our concern. We were driven back with the steel tips of bayonets poking us in our chests.

While we shared the good luck of not being strafed by our own planes, along with the joy of watching the "Oryoku Maru" sink to the bottom, the Japanese were determined to make sure we would never again delight in such pleasures. Angered by their losses, and determined, now more than ever, to get the strongest of us to Japan, they put the next part of their plan into action.

By December 15th, the day we were crowded onto the tennis courts, we had lost two hundred and seventy- nine men. Our treatment over the coming days guaranteed that number would only increase.

For the first four days, we were given no food. The water spigot ran at a constant trickle. Five men died. Surprisingly, Major Swanson, seemed to be improving.

On the 5th, 6th, and 7th day of our continuing saga, we each received a meager three tablespoons of uncooked rice. Horrible as it was, with all of us starving, we forced ourselves to eat it.

The next day, half of us were placed on a truck convoy, thirty-five men standing on the back of each truck. On our feet for over six hours, we crossed the Zanbales Mountains, finally arriving at our destination of San Fernando, Pampango Province. Here, along with the most seriously ill and injured men, we were placed in the city jail and its surrounding courtyard.

Overnight the trucks returned to Subic Bay to pick up the remainder of the men. When they returned to San Fernando they were placed in an old abandoned theater, the plaster peeling and the seats ripped out. The only source of water, a leaky toilet.

Over the next three or four days we received very small portions of steamed rice. In "celebration" of Christmas we were each given one bowl of vegetable soup. Mr. Wada Shunsuke, the Japanese interpreter assigned to prisoners, approached the Commander of the jail. He proposed the Japanese transport fifteen of the most seriously injured men back to Manila for hospitalization. These men were chosen and placed on trucks provided by the Japanese.

Unbeknownst to us, rather than heading to Manila, the trucks drove to a small cemetery on the outskirts of town. They were met by a half dozen Japanese soldiers gathered around a hole in the ground, twenty feet square by four feet deep. Two guards took one POW at a time, ordered him to kneel at the edge of the hole, and bayoneted him in the back. Each was then decapitated, his body pushed into the gravesite.

As the prisoners were on their way to the cemetery, back at the theater, Jack Kaster passed away. Badly wounded on the "Hell Ship", he never let on the extent of his injuries to the Japanese for fear of retaliation. A very good friend was now gone! What a bunch of ....

Among the men killed that night at the cemetery were LTC Ulysses J.L. Peoples, a West Point graduate and ordnance officer, and Pharmacist 2/C Deenah R. McCurry, a young Navy corpsman who had volunteered to make the trip to Manila to provide what physical comfort he could for the prisoners.

Most distressing was that Doctor Swanson, our mentor, our father figure, the man who gave us what little hope we had, was one of the fifteen slaughtered that day by the miserable Japanese bastards. One of the most respected men we knew, the man who was the glue that held us together, certainly never deserved such a horrific death. His loss was devastating to us all and left us grief stricken and defeated. Farewell, Doctor Swanson!

Chapter Twenty-Four

Aboard the "Enoura" & "Brazil Maru"
As Remembered by
1st. Lt. Paul George

Christmas Eve morning, we were brought from the theater and jail and marched a half mile to the town railroad station. Reminiscent of our days traveling toward Cabanatuan, we were once again packed into very small Filipino style freight cars, one hundred and ten men to a car. The Japanese were so short of cars, they even placed twenty more prisoners on top of each car.

Many suspected the Japanese were abandoning their plans to purge Luzon of prisoners due to the difficulties they had encountered thus far. As bad as we thought conditions had been, we would have been elated to be returning to either Bilibid or Cabanatuan. Within a short time, we figured out we were traveling northwest toward the Lingayen Gulf, not southeast toward Manila. Much to our chagrin, we were inching our way towards Japan.

On Christmas day, we arrived at another San Fernando, on the west coast of Luzon. For two days, we endured extremely hot days followed by very cold nights on the beaches surrounding the port.

All of us had discarded our shoes and most of our clothing while abandoning the "Oryoku Maru" and swimming to shore. Most of us had on nothing more than our undershorts.

On the beach, food was scarce, water unavailable, and shelter nonexistent. We received one rice ball and four to five tablespoons of water on the evening of the second day. We used the sand for a blanket.

Waiting those two days, we watched as the convoy we were about to board grew from two to eight vessels, including two small destroyers as escorts. Activity in the harbor became very hectic. Thousands of troops were offloaded onto barges and tugs that carried them to small piers close to shore. Guns, mortars, small artillery pieces, and pack horses with munition boxes all confirmed the Japanese were gearing up for a horrendous fight; where it would take place, we did not know.

Abruptly, long before dawn on December 27th, the remaining one thousand three hundred and twenty-eight of us were roused from our sleep, and quickly placed on harbor boats. We were then shuttled to a waiting transport with a big white "ONE" painted on her stack. With most of us already on board, two hundred of the most seriously injured and ill were still climbing over the rails onto the ship. The "Enoura Maru", as it was known, anxious to stay on schedule, together with an escort, hoisted her anchors and set sail.

Realizing the consequences of inaction, the Captain of the barge sped toward yet another transport with our men still boarding. This ship had "Two" painted on its stack. It was called the "Brazil Maru". Literally, the injured and ill men were quickly pushed over the rail of the barge onto the second transport as it, also, was pulling away.

The "Brazil Maru" was an old tub, at least twenty-five years old. A coal burning ship, weighing ten tons she could only travel at ten knots per hour. She was in very poor shape, full of rust and filthy.

Carrying fewer than two hundred and fifty prisoners, at least this ship was far from crowded. We could lie down to rest or sleep. Having carried horses from the Philippines, however, lying in straw deep with muck that had not been raked for the entire trip, was most unappealing.

An even bigger problem with the "Brazil Maru" was that she was ill equipped for passengers. Returning to Japan empty, with no cargo or troops, she was staffed with a crew of only ten. Food and water were barely adequate to sustain them. Nonetheless, after two days of us going without, the sailors began to share what little they had. Remarkably, because of their generosity and our first touch of humanity in years, only five men died during the entire trip.

We reached Takao Harbor on southern Formosa on New Year's Day along with the "Enoura Maru". We were kept on our respective ships until January 7th. We were fed occasionally, and provided very little water. Between the 7th and the 9th, men from the "Brazil Maru" were transferred by tugs to the "Enoura Maru". This was all done in preparation for the final leg of the journey to Japan, as originally planned.

Of the fifty or sixty ships in the harbor on the 9th, all were anchored by themselves, except for one barge unloading its cargo of sugar onto the "Enoura Maru". Suddenly, two dive-bombers appeared. To increase their odds of hitting their target, they swooped down on the only two ships tied together in the harbor. Bombs struck the barge and the "Enoura's" forward hold killing two hundred and thirty-eight of the four hundred and fifty-two prisoners. Twenty men in the number two hold were also killed. Many more prisoners were wounded.

It quickly became obvious that "thinning the herd" was once again in vogue. Over the next three days we received no food, water, or honey buckets. There certainly was no medical attention.

BRAZIL MARU – 300 Killed

On the afternoon of the 12th, the Japanese finally gave permission to remove the dead from the ship. By now, sixty more men had died, including Bill Bianchi. He became one of the three hundred and eighteen naked bodies stacked crisscross beneath the hatch; a truly horrendous site. He was my last hope of my getting out of this war and home alive, and I was devastated by the thought. I hated that he was gone. He wasn't just an Army buddy. He had become like a brother to me. It was like I'd lost a family member to a bunch of murdering animals.!

It was then that I witnessed the most repulsive action that would sicken even the heartiest of men. A rope, tied around the ankles, hoisted each man topside, blood and feces dripping from their dangling hands. To witness these guys being hauled up like a fish on a hook made me sick to my stomach.

Once on deck, the bodies were placed in cargo nets, and taken over the side to waiting barges. Accompanied by a detail of American prisoners, they were taken to the beach at Takao Harbor. Here, with the detail too weak to carry the bodies, they were dragged up the beach by the rope already tied around their ankles and delivered to the Japanese for mass burial. A salute by their comrades was their final farewell.

In the eyes of the Japanese, these several hundred Americans had finally received their due justice for disgracefully surrendering. In the mind of every American watching was, "There, but for the grace of God, go I"!

Chapter Twenty-Five

Welcome to Japan
According to
1st. Lt. Paul George

On the afternoon of the 13th of January, the eight hundred and ten surviving prisoners from the now completely scuttled "Enoura Maru" were transferred to the "Brazil Maru". Coal for fuel loaded on board, she cast off for Japan that very evening. She was the oldest and most unkempt ship in the Japanese fleet of five cargo ships and two small warships. It was a wonder she was still seaworthy.

The "Brazil Maru" frequently dropped anchor during the day to avoid enemy aircraft. At night because of submarine activity, she hid by sailing between the islands. For days, we towed a crippled ship hit by a torpedo, reducing our speed even further.

♣♣♣♣♣♣

No longer in the tropics, the weather grew increasingly colder. All clothing was removed from corpses and redistributed. With constant sleet and snow and temperatures well below freezing at night, we were forced to huddle close together for warmth. Pneumonia began to cause as many deaths as starvation once had.

Scanty tee-shirts and shorts helped no one. Each morning the twenty or so men who had died during the night from exposure were stacked for lifting topside. Each night the bodies of these men were pushed overboard.

We arrived at Moji, Japan on January 29th. The average sailing time from Formosa to Japan was five days. Our trip took the "Brazil Maru" seventeen. During the trip food was practically nonexistent, water measured only in teaspoons. Conditions were deplorable.

We began the journey with eight hundred and ten men. We completed it with four hundred and twenty-five. We lost three hundred and eighty-five men in less than three weeks, and one thousand, one hundred and ninety-four since sailing on the "Oryuko Maru". Unbelievable!

♣♣♣♣♣♣

During the trip from Formosa I didn't feel at all well. My beriberi was causing tremendous swelling in my legs, along with severe shortness of breath. I had a slight belly-ache, but I wrote that off as dehydration.

When we arrived at Fukuoka Number Three POW Camp we walked a mere four hundred yards from the bay to the city of Tobata. Here, we all scrambled to find a room in one of the ten, two stories, shabbily built barracks. The floors were concrete. We all had a straw mattress for sleeping. A little shelf at the head of the mattress held our personnel belongings, what few we had.

Each barrack contained a concrete urinal, six wooden stall latrines with a large tank beneath and sinks with cold running, contaminated, water. We were cautioned not to drink the water!

There was a building with two ten-foot square by three feet deep concrete tubs, hot water for bathing, and a mess hall with rice pots and tanks for making tea. We were allowed seven hundred and fifty calories a day, well below the three thousand required each day to maintain working weight. Officers, while not required to work, were enticed to do so by reducing their allowance to five hundred calories a day, if they refused.

♣♣♣♣♣♣

We traveled thirty minutes each way, seven days a week, on open carts to work in the Yahati Steel Mills in the city of Yawata. All the steel mills and rolling plants were producing Japanese war materials utilizing only POW slave labor to manufacture them.

For each working day of nine to ten hours, pay was a mere fifty cents a month. Cigarettes, like at Cabanatuan, were barter. Officers were given ten each week, enlisted men thirty. Two "smokes" could buy two spoonsful of rice or half a cup of soup. For the non-smoker, again, that became a very good deal.

My first day of work, primarily as a Stevedore, completely wiped me out. The next day, I was listed as "sick in quarters" and given reduced rations, along with a little "knuckle therapy" from a few of the guards. I forced myself to return to work the following day.

Each night, I began to have beautiful, vivid dreams; and thankfully, no nightmares. In one dream, the three guys and I were walking down Knob Hill in San Francisco arm in arm with smiles from ear to ear. We had just returned from overseas on a luxury liner. We were clean shaved, had gotten haircuts, showered and were issued the newest, best pressed uniforms available. We each proudly displayed a full chest of medals. Bill was wearing his Congressional Medal of Honor around his neck, and glowing with pride. We had all just been promoted, put on some weight, and looked extremely healthy.

Jack was talking about heading for El Paso to rejoin his wife Susan. He was looking forward to rejoining the family funeral business. Doctor Swanson was meeting his wife Maude at the Denver Rail Station. They were going to take the slowest, most leisurely train trip to Washington, D.C. where he was assigned to Walter Reed Army Hospital. In addition to resuming his professional career, Maude and he were planning to start a family.

Bill was heading to Minnesota to begin his life once again with his Mom and sisters. I was meeting my brother, William, in San Diego to help him run the resort he took over when Mom died. Sounds like we all had our lives well planned, doesn't it?

I worked again the third day, but felt even worse. I was extremely thirsty, got dizzy when I stood up, and was severely fatigued. I had absolutely no appetite at all.

I had another great dream that night! I was with a gal I had dated in college. We were sitting on a couch in front of a nice warm fireplace listening to Big Band music. Guys like Glenn Miller playing "Pennsylvania 6-5000", Benny Goodman, the "King of Swing", and Tommy Dorsey, the "Sentimental Gentleman of Swing". Just cuddling with an occasional smooch. It was great!

When I awoke, I could barely move. The Japanese diagnosed me with acute enteritis, an inflammation of the small bowel and dehydration. I was immediately placed in the hospital. By now I had a very painful abdomen. I received intravenous glucose for the dehydration, but nothing to manage the pain.

All I remember is that I wanted to sleep. The pain got worse and at times unbearable. I dreamed of the guys again and again, asking their forgiveness for ignoring them saying over and over, "I'm just very, very tired....Please, just let me sleep....Please, just let me sleep.....Please, just let me sleep"!

Part Five

Obituaries

El Paso Herald-Post

March 14, 1945

KASTER, John Lafferty "Jack"

John Kaster "Jack" 32, 1st. Lt. US Army of Wheeling St., El Paso, TX, was reported killed in action on December 28, 1944 on Luzon, Philippine Islands. His remains are interred in the Manila American Cemetery and Memorial within the boundaries of Fort William McKinley, Manila, Philippine Islands.

Lt. Kaster was preceded in death by his father, James. He is survived by his mother, Maude, his wife, Susan, a daughter, Hester Suzanne, and a brother, James, all of El Paso.

Lt. Kaster graduated from the University of Arizona in 1934 with a BS and BA in Business Administration. He went on to join the staff of the family owned and operated funeral business eventually becoming vice-president overseeing the casket portion of the company.

Lt. Kaster was assigned as company commander and supply officer with the 7th Materials Squadron at Fort Stoltenberg, Philippines. Captured by the Japanese in April 1942, he was forced to make the notorious Bataan Death March. He was imprisoned in several filthy and extremely brutal POW camps for some 40 months, and then sailed on the "Hell Ship", "Oryoku Maru", toward Japan. Pilots from the USS Hornet, unaware of "passengers" on the unmarked ship, bombed and sank it killing 942 unsuspecting American POWs. Lt. Kaster was seriously injured and died a few weeks later on 12/29/44.

As the misfortunes of war rained down upon this young officer, with the highest hopes for his professional and family life, he faced challenges with a gusto unknown to most. Likewise, he took what the war handed out, and pushed back hard against the "Hells" that few were able to endure.

San Diego Evening Tribune   February 28, 1949

GEORGE, Jr., Paul, Theodore

Paul T. George, Jr., 29, 1st. Lt. US Army, of Granada St., San Diego, CA. died on February 8, 1945, and was buried at the Manila American Cemetery and Memorial within the boundaries of Fort William McKinley, Manila, Philippine Islands. He was today being returned to his family and reentered in the Fort Rosecrans National Cemetery, San Diego.

Lt. George was preceded in death by his father, Paul, Sr., and his mother Mary E. He is survived by a brother William G. and his sister-in-law Mildred of Quincy, Oregon.

Lt. George graduated with a BA in Psychology from the University of California in 1937. He served as a reservist with the 7th Materials Squadron until June when he was called to active duty. Following basic training he was assigned as mess officer for the unit at Clark Field on Luzon, Philippine Islands.

Lt. George was captured by the Japanese and forced to make the Bataan Death March on which over 5,000 Americans were slaughtered; imprisoned in overcrowded POW camps where 30,000 men were executed or starved to death; and forced to take three "Hell Ships", two of which were sunk by unsuspecting American dive-bombers. Total, on all the "Hell Ships" torpedoed or bombed during the war, 21,000 American prisoners were killed by friendly fire.

Lt. George spent his final days as a patient in the Fukuoka POW hospital on the island of Kyushu in Japan. Here, he died of beriberi and acute enteritis caused by malnutrition and dehydration.

Many men made trips through all three "Hells" that Lt. George faced before they met their Maker. This was a journey that no man should have ever had to endure.

New Ulm Review   March 10, 1947

BIANCHI, Willibald "Bill"

Willibald, Bianchi, "Bill", 29, 1st. Lt. US Army of 1st. North Street, New Ulm, MN. was today reentered at the Honolulu Hawaii National Cemetery of the Pacific (Punchbowl). His remains were recovered as part of a mass grave of 311 Americans buried in Takao, Formosa on January 9, 1945.

Lt. Bianchi was preceded in death by his father, Joseph. He is survived by his mother, Caroline, and four sisters, Josephine, Germaine, Magdalene, and Mary Louise, all of new Ulm.

Lt. Bianchi graduated in 1939 with a BS in Agricultural Studies from South Dakota State University having been awarded a full ROTC academic scholarship. By 1940 he had received his commission as an Army officer. Following basic training and extensive combat training he began his first assignment as Commander, D Company, Philippine Scouts, 45th Infantry, in Bagac, on the Bataan Peninsula, Philippine Islands.

On February 3, 1942, Lt. Bianchi was involved in a military action for which he would later be awarded the Congressional Medal of Honor. However, two months later he was forced to surrender, made the frightful Bataan Death March, was imprisoned for yeas in dreadful POW camps, and traveled aboard horrifying "Hell Ships". After surviving the "Oryoku Maru" he was killed by unsuspecting American dive-bomber pilots while on board the "Enoura Maru".

Lt. Bianchi was a hero not only in life, but also in death.

Maryville Enterprise   October 21, 1945

SWANSON, M.D., Wendell, Fleet

Wendell F. Swanson, M.D., 41, Major, US Army of Washington Pike, Knoxville, TN. was declared killed in action on December 23rd, on Luzon, Philippine Islands. His remains are interred at the Manila American Cemetery and Memorial within the boundaries of Fort William McKinley, Manila, Philippine Islands.

Major Swanson is survived by his wife, Maude of Alabama, his parents James L. and Daisy K., two brothers, Wayne and Willard, and two sisters, Winona and Worth, all of Knoxville, TN.

Major Swanson obtained his bachelors and medical degrees from the University of Tennessee at Memphis. He enlisted in the US Army and completed his internship and general surgery residency with an emphasis on trauma at Fitzsimmons General Hospital in Denver, CO. His first assignment in mid-1940 was at Fort Mills General Hospital on Corregidor, Philippine Islands.

Following the surrender of Corregidor to the Japanese in May 1942, Maj. Swanson was captured and briefly confined at Bilibid Prison followed by over three years at Camp Cabanatuan. During transport to Japan to be used as slave labor, the unmarked "Hell Ship" he was aboard, the "Oryoku Maru", was sunk by Navy dive bombers. He survived the sinking, but was seriously wounded.

About a week later, under the pretense of returning to Manila for medical care by the Japanese, he and fourteen other gravely wounded soldiers were taken to a nearby cemetery, made to kneel at the side of a mass grave, executed, beheaded, and pushed into the grave.

Major Swanson, who had dedicated his life to saving others, made the ultimate sacrifice by giving his life for his Country.

www.ingramcontent.com/pod-product-compliance
Lightning Source LLC
Chambersburg PA
CBHW072358030726
47505CB00014B/1883